THE THIRD (

DAVID F. CASE was born in upstate New York in 1937, but lived most of his adult life in London, as well as spending time in Greece and Spain. His acclaimed collection *The Cell: Three Tales of Horror* appeared in 1969, and it was followed by the novels *Fengriffen: A Chilling Tale*, *Wolf Tracks* and *The Third Grave*. His other collections include *Brotherly Love and Other Tales of Trust and Knowledge*, *Pelican Cay & Other Disquieting Tales*, and an omnibus volume in the *Masters of the Weird Tale* series from Centipede Press. A regular contributor to the legendary *Pan Book of Horror Stories* during the early 1970s, his powerful zombie novella "Pelican Cay" in *Dark Terrors 5* was nominated for a World Fantasy Award in 2001. He died in 2018.

DAVID CASE

THE THIRD GRAVE

VALANCOURT BOOKS

The Third Grave by David Case
Originally published by Arkham House in 1981
First Valancourt Books edition 2019

Published by Valancourt Books
http://www.valancourtbooks.com

ISBN 978-1-948405-38-6 (trade paperback)

Also available as an electronic book.

All Valancourt Books publications are printed on acid free paper that
meets all ANSI standards for archival quality paper.

Cover by David Moscati
Set in Dante MT

Place me among the stars imperishable . . .
that I may not die.

—Pyramid Text

Knowing Mallory but slightly, I was surprised when his letter arrived at the cottage. The day had been foul: the sky was drab with undefined clouds, and the rain careened wildly in the wind. The unhappy postman trudged down the path with his shoulders hunched, pushing his bicycle before him, and as he placed the letter in my box, hurled a malevolent glance at the house as if he resented the detour. Not much caring for unexpected correspondence, I returned his rebuke as I retrieved the communication. It had been addressed to me in care of the museum and forwarded from there, obviously the logical —if not the only—way to contact me. I didn't recognize the handwriting and turned over the envelope. On the flap was the return address of Lucian Mallory.

I hadn't the faintest idea why he should be writing to me. I'd encountered the man on two occasions, both rather exotic, some four years before. Since then I had heard nothing of him. I took the letter to the fireside and pondered over it for a few moments while the wind laced the corners of the cottage and howled in the chimney. Thinking of Mallory reminded me of a different time, in a region where the wind was dry with stinging sand and an English rain would have been most welcome indeed.

I first met Lucian Mallory in the wilderness above the Great Cataract during the time I was attached to Sir Harold Gregory's archaeological dig at that site. It had been thought, although this proved a disappointment, that a great quantity of hieratic writing would be uncovered there, and the museum had enlisted my services to render on-the-spot translations. There had been a few recent blunders in which archaeologists, proceeding with inordinate haste, had unbalanced their findings by their own efforts, and it was hoped that my translations might be of immediate value in determining which directions to follow as the subsequent layers were uncovered. This made a certain degree of sense. It was a shame that artifacts which had rested undisturbed through the ages should, in the moment of discovery, have their continuity disrupted.

Although well known in his field, Sir Harold himself was no scholar. He was an interested amateur who, through a felicitous combination of private income and unprofessional zeal, had achieved some success and considerable reclame. Unable to translate his own findings or to comprehend their true significance, but quite prepared to finance grandiose expeditions, Sir Harold was rather more interested in enhancing his reputation than in casting light on mankind's clouded past. Nonetheless, I didn't resent the man. Whatever his motivation, he was responsible for some impressive discoveries, and vanity has ever been a driving force both in the forging of history and in understanding it afterward. Needless to say, I welcomed the opportunity to work with him in the field.

Perhaps as an idealistic young scholar I had expected too much.

After three months I became disheartened. The everyday regimen of such a project requires patience and dedication, and meager results are the rule. We slaved under a sun too hot to be contained, spreading incandescent watercolors across the sky. We lived in tents. Sand seeped into the very marrow of our bones. Sir Harold became cross and irritable, possibly considering our lack of results a slur upon his judgment. But to his credit he persevered, and in the end we made a notable find. Shaving off the side of a cliff, millimeter by millimeter as it were, we unearthed a New Kingdom sarcophagus containing a particularly fine mummy that had been sequestered within a rock-cut tomb.

The mummy, a small male swathed in dry resinous linen, was very well preserved, its hands folded over its sunken breast in an attitude of perpetual repose. Apparently a priest or minor official of the Twentieth Dynasty, our specimen had been interred with the customary funerary accoutrements —amulets, canopic jars, ushabtis—and was still faintly redolent of the aromatic unguents applied in his entombment. I felt a twinge of man's unholiness when we disturbed that timeless slumber and suppose that such momentary regrets, though vestigial, are natural. Sir Harold was overjoyed. I had more interest in the sarcophagus, for it was etched on all sides with hierograms and symbols and would provide many days of fruitful study. I set to my labors; Sir Harold immediately notified the Egyptian Department of Antiquities and the Director-General of the Cairo Museum. He seemed to regard the mummy as a beneficent friend and in the days that followed was often seen sitting beside the sarcophagus, his arms folded in animate echo of the mummy. Several times I was given the impression he would have liked to shake its hand and congratulate it on being found.

Then Mallory appeared in the camp.

My initial impression of the man is singular.

At first I took him to be an Arab, for he wore a hooded djellaba and entered the camp astride a camel, staring intently ahead with the arrogance of the nomad. Behind him came another man, obviously unhappy with his beast's gait. The second stranger was a European, and I assumed that the first was his guide.

Sir Harold Gregory advanced to meet them, appearing puzzled, and the robed figure sprang lightly to the ground. He faced Gregory, a tall gaunt man in flowing robes, and I noticed that he wore well-polished boots, which seemed strange footwear for a native. In the next instant I saw that he was not a native, for he threw back his cowl with an abrupt snap of his head, revealing an extraordinary countenance. This was

Lucian Mallory. His face was lean with sunken cheeks and shaped like a wedge, as if his maker had fashioned it with frontal blows of an axe. His eyes were astonishing, set so deeply in their bony sockets that he seemed to have no lateral vision —when he wished to look to either side, he turned his whole head; turning only his eyes, he saw but the ledges of his skull.

"I am Lucian Mallory," he intoned. His voice was well suited to his face.

"Er, Gregory," said our leader.

"Yes, I recognized you, Sir Harold."

Gregory was pleased.

"I've heard of your recent find," Mallory said. "Since my own work lies in a parallel field—although not as well known as yours, I fear—and since my present efforts have brought me to this area, I thought it both my pleasure and my duty to call and offer my congratulations."

"Very kind of you, sir."

"Perhaps you've heard of me?"

Sir Harold was obviously discomforted; it was apparent he had no idea who Mallory was and equally apparent that he didn't wish to offend the fellow. He creased his aristocratic brow and delved for memory, then politely groped for some inspired inconsequentiality.

"Mallory? Mallory? I do believe—"

Mallory championed Sir Harold's veracity with a timely gesture dismissing the question: "No matter, no matter. Fame is a fleeting virtue; perhaps no virtue at all, to men such as we, Sir Harold. Perhaps, indeed, fame serves only to hinder one's more noble efforts, is it not so?"

Mallory smiled slightly.

"Just so," agreed Sir Harold.

Not a subtle gentleman, Sir Harold did not look for the shaded thrust of nuance in others; not an unintelligent man, secure within himself, he possessed the outstanding ability to fail to recognize rather than to react. I felt this served him well.

During this colloquy the second stranger remained astride his camel, slumped and awkward. Mallory now turned to him and nodded. It was a motion of permission, and the man dismounted heavily with a sigh of relief. He was a very large chap, built along powerful rectangular lines, a monolith in contrast to Mallory's obelisk. His solid face was angry with sunburn, and his khaki shirt clung to his torso in concentric swirls of sweat. He stood just behind Mallory, a paradigm of menial solicitude. Mallory did not see fit to introduce him.

"You'll want to see our mummy, eh?" Gregory inquired.

"I'd hoped to, yes."

"We've given the old boy his own quarters," Sir Harold explained. "If you'll come this way—"

I was seated outside my tent, under the awning, working at my field desk. The mummy was kept in a separate tent, and as Gregory led Mallory toward it they passed close before me. Gregory paused and introduced us. Mallory offered me a dry look and a nod. They moved on, and I watched as Sir Harold threw open the sarcophagus with a theatrical gesture, like a barker displaying some exhibit in a carnival sideshow. Mallory leaned forward from the waist, his hands clasped behind his back. He was saying something and nodding. In the shadow of the canvas his eyes receded even farther into their sockets, and yet even at a distance I saw them glitter in cold pinpoints, like small rodents residing within a skull.

By this time it was late in the afternoon, and Sir Harold quite naturally asked Mallory if he would remain the night in our camp. He agreed but announced that he would make his own arrangements for dining. This seemed at first a polite gesture toward occasioning no inconvenience, and Gregory insisted it would not trouble us. Mallory replied that in such matters he had his own style, as he termed it, and was adamant in his refusal to join us. He then issued instructions to his companion. I had wondered about that fellow's function and now saw that he was a general manservant, a sort of butler-in-the-rough. He proceeded to unpack several articles from the camels while Mallory disappeared into the tent Sir Harold had assigned them for the night.

An astonishing ritual followed. We had fallen into the habit of living rather primitively at the camp, but Lucian Mallory, his Arabian dress notwithstanding, obviously had his own ideas about life in the field. I watched, intrigued, as his man erected an aluminum folding table and covered it with an immaculate white linen cloth. He then, very correctly, arranged on the table a silver place setting complete even to candlesticks. This accomplished, he prepared dinner, and just as the first course was ready, Mallory emerged from the tent in a white dinner jacket. Everyone in camp was watching by this time, but Mallory seemed serenely unaware of our interest. He seated himself, and his servant attended him just as though they'd been in a dining room at the Savoy.

It was both laughable and admirable to see Mallory at his elegant table in those great trackless wastes, and I hardly knew what to think. The obvious inference was that Mallory was one of those men so bound by tradition that he simply could not alter his behavior in accord with circumstances, but a moment's reflection dispelled this supposition, for he certainly had adapted to the extent of wearing native attire. I finally concluded that he simply enjoyed the form of tradition without being welded to its substance. This seemed commendable, and I resolved to get to know Mallory at the earliest opportunity.

He ate with variety, but sparsely, and when the meal was finished and his man had cleared the table, I wandered over. Mallory was enjoying a cigar and brandy and offered me the same. Scholarly asceticism aside, I eagerly accepted.

"Sam," he said, and motioned.

His servant brought another chair. I hesitated for a moment, glancing down at my rough clothing, divorced for a second from reality. Tradition is a clinging affair, and even here, with the wilderness stretching away on all sides and the evening wind beginning to rise, I felt the impropriety of sitting, dressed as I was, at that elegant table. Mallory was observing me with amusement. I laughed and sat down. Both cigar and brandy were of the highest quality.

"You do yourself well," I said.

"Well enough."

"It seems rather paradoxical."

"Why is that?"

He regarded me across the rim of his glass.

"This gracious manner—in the desert."

"Oh?"

"Surely you see that?"

"I see that I dine as suits me best. We all have our styles, young man."

His tone was condescending, and I replied somewhat annoyed, "I would have thought you'd be better advised to use all the pack space available for your equipment."

"I have all the equipment I require. Indeed I don't find actual tools very helpful."

He knew I was surprised at this statement and drew on his cigar while watching me through the smoke. The candle was still lighted, flickering in the wind, illuminating his face with elongated angles. The tents were starting to snap, and the trackless sands were creeping around the camp. Instead of replying to Mallory, I looked out at the dunes. Imperceptibly but inexorably the sands shifted, registering the passage of aeons, an hourglass of planetary dimensions.

"Unless, of course, you consider the mind a tool—"

I turned back to my host. "Of course. A very functional tool."

"Yes. I admire the human mind. As opposed to the brain, you understand. But there is your paradox for you. To study the mind, one must employ the mind. That's hardly true of the more mundane tools." He paused, then continued. "Perhaps I've given the impression that I'm an archaeologist. That isn't exact. I'm studying the past, yes, but not as past. Time has no dominion in my studies. Mankind moves through history as a fish moves through water, and time, like the seas, is a fluid constant."

"Are you suggesting a new physics or a new philosophy?" Mallory laughed.

"Let us suggest—a new science."

"But how is it connected to Egyptology?"

"Why, in the way that all things living are connected: the sorrowful bond of mortality, the regrettable arrangement whereby the fine instrument of the mind is hopelessly held captive within the corruptible brain. The mind is capable of immortality, you understand. It is only the body that must decay." He paused and looked at me, as if to ascertain whether I was following his rather recondite reasoning. His eyes, peering straight ahead from the depressions of his skull, had a resolute and penetrating gaze. I suddenly realized what was so disturbing about them; set as they were, capable only of frontal vision, Mallory's optics were constructed like a carnivore, like some great hunting cat which peers straight ahead to judge distance rather than a herbivore which, eyes divided, can search for predators on both sides. This was a fanciful notion, of course, and yet it was striking; his conversation was aggressive and predatory. He attacked with verbal talons.

I resolved to be no helpless victim and, looking back at him, observed, "That is all very well and good, and presumably there is some value in theoretical—not to say, theological—musings, but it hardly answers my question, sir." I was rather pleased with myself for this statement and drew on my cigar to conceal an urge to smile. I had decided he was an amateur Renaissance man—or perceived himself as such—spreading himself thin in an age of specialization.

"Just what is your question?" he asked.

"Just what is your field of study?"

"Ah, how typical. You wish to categorize me, just as you catalog ancient urns and assign a chronology to the dynasties and, yes, desecrate the tombs of the dead. Don't you see that, by fashioning a static knowledge, you lose the feel of reality? That by simplifying facts on charts and graphs, you alter those facts in the process?"

"Knowledge must have some form."

Mallory sighed.

"I expect it must," he said. "So must magic, for that matter. So be it. I'll satisfy your curiosity. I am interested in chemistry and have some medical learning. You will think that a strange background for an Egyptologist."

"Is it not?"

"Only by narrowing concepts. The ancients had a well-developed chemistry."

"I can't accept that, sir. They had made a rudimentary beginning, agreed."

Mallory continued imperturbably, "Even our word 'chemistry' is derived from the old Egyptian word *kemt.*"

I raised my eyebrows. He was intruding upon my field here, and without seeming too smug, I replied, "A tenuous derivation at best. *Kemt,* as I'm sure you know, meant 'black land.' The ancients had only a slight practical knowledge, strongly tinged with magic; they learned rather a lot about anatomy and drugs as an unintended concomitant to their religion. They dissected and mummified corpses, and naturally acquired knowledge as a side effect. The goal was not science, however. These matters are interesting to us in helping to understand the past, but they had no learning which could possibly be of value to a modern student of chemistry. Unless, perhaps, you believe that the properties and behavior of elements can be somehow affected by the chanting of incantations?"

"What do you know of it?" he snapped.

"As much as most men, I daresay."

"Agreed. And do you suppose that most men know anything at all? Now or then?"

"I don't follow you."

"If there was an advanced science in the past, do you expect that the common man was versed in it? That he even knew it existed? Mankind hasn't changed, and knowledge has ever been reserved for the few. Today there exists a handful of scientists who understand the atom, who can direct a spacecraft to the moon. But to the average man, such knowledge is meaningless. It was the same in the past. The difference, and only by our subsequent definitions, is that the ancients thought of the knowledge denied them as magic, and today we call it science. No difference at all, really. Will you accept that?"

I shrugged. "Of course."

"Well, then. It is that secret knowledge for which I am looking. It is not buried as deeply as you might presume. Granted it revolved around religion and death, but that does not preclude value. It enhances it, rather, for all life revolves around —and gravitates toward—death. What is a man, after all, but a corpse supported by a soul?"

"A nice phrase. Have you made any progress?"

"Some. A beginning." He frowned. "I'm hampered by the fact that my knowledge does not include a command of old Egyptian; that I require help with certain translations. I do understand demotic Egyptian, but—"

"I would have thought it more valuable to have studied the old language."

"Yes, you would," he muttered. "Just as you think it more appropriate to live like a savage while you're here in the desert. Does it not occur to you that the pharaohs lived a life of luxury? That, by denying oneself the pleasures of life, one erects a stark hindrance to understanding the kings of former ages? You study the past for the sake of the past, regarding it as a puzzle, an abstract proposition to be probed with cold instruments." He paused and shook his head. "That limited viewpoint blinds you. My work is in the present. I wish to bring a sense of immediacy to bear on these findings of another time. Men lived then, and they died. They had their hopes, their dreams, their thoughts and fears. To see them as withered mummies is to take a one-dimensional attitude. One should rather make dynamic studies."

"Poetic, sir. But scientific?"

"More than you can know."

"Can you tell me more?"

He scowled and replied portentously, "You may waste your time on crumbling ruins if you like. I prefer to know the life that passed through those ruins in their time of glory. You may value an ancient writing because the papyruses are durable; because the scroll is an object from the past. I care nothing for objects. I want to know the knowledge contained in that writing, the secret meaning in the obscure symbols. The eternal truths, if you will."

"All very admirable," I said. My cigar was finished, my glass empty. I rose from the table. Mallory shrugged, as if the gesture could serve as a dismissal, and so it did. I thought him a strange man indeed.

After leaving Mallory, I worked some time on the inscriptions surrounding the winged disk of the sarcophagus and then, as was my habit, took a brisk walk. I found the exercise a good method of clearing away the thoughts of the day before attempting sleep and also enjoyed the fanciful mood of adventure that is always present in the desert. I strolled past the excavation and then along the base of the escarpment, keeping the lights of the camp in sight. The land rose gradually here, converging toward the top of the cliff at an elongated angle with the sand jammed in against the weathered rock. Peering out over the landscape, I saw that the entire desert had become suffused with a silvery lunar radiance; the rugged terrain subdued, the shrubs and small trees transformed into apparitions of mystic beauty. I paused to fill my pipe and then light it, with some difficulty in the dry wind. The smoke was torn from the bowl and shredded away in the distance. As I stood there a figure approached, and in a moment I recognized Mallory's servant. He halted beside me.

"Enjoyin' a walk, sir?"

"Good evening, Sam."

"A good thing to stretch the old legs after spendin' a day on that blasted camel," he said. "If ever God has made a worthless beast, it's the camel."

"It takes a while to get used to their gait, eh?"

"It does that. And the smell, that's the worst part. Did you know, sir, that goats have been known to faint at the odor of the camel's breath?"

I smiled.

"I didn't know that, no."

"It's the God's honest truth."

"Have you been in Egypt long?"

"Why, I was here durin' the war, you know."

"Is that so?"

"Yes," he grunted. "Fightin' the malignant Hun. That's what Churchill called them, you know, sir. Malignant Huns. I reckon that's pretty correct. Yes, sir, I was here then and I'm here now and I didn't like it then and I don't like it now. Still, a man has to go where his duty and his work takes him, and there's nothin' to be done for it." Sam shrugged. "The cities now, Cairo and all, they are a bit all right. It's this bloody desert that isn't fit for mankind. I was always afraid I'd be killed here. During the war, I mean. I wasn't afraid of gettin' killed itself, you know. It was just that I didn't fancy bein' buried here in Egypt. Imagine bein' buried here? Lord! The least a man can expect is to be buried in England, where there's a bit of life, wouldn't you say, sir?"

I laughed.

"Well, that's life," he said.

"Have you been with Mallory long?"

"A few years now. Cooper's my name. Sam Cooper."

We shook hands.

"I imagine Mallory is a difficult man to work for?"

"Oh, it's not so bad."

"He's an—interesting fellow."

"Aye. A man of genius. Peculiar maybe, but a genius."

"Has he made any discoveries recently?"

"Things, sir, such as you've never dreamed."

"I don't suppose you can be specific?"

Sam looked at me and scratched his head.

"I'm not at liberty to talk about that," he said. Then he broke into a wide grin. "Truth is, I don't really understand much of it, anyhow. Take some understanding these things do. I only know they are things of genius."

I nodded, deciding that Mallory had completely dumbfounded the man, that he had a disciple, rather than a servant, and that undoubtedly was just the way Mallory wished it. We talked for a few minutes longer and then strolled back to the camp together. I retired to my tent then and slept soundly, and when I awoke in the morning, Mallory and his man already had departed. I did not think about Mallory at that time, however, for I had awakened under unusual circumstances; I had, in fact, been suddenly roused by Sir Harold's cry of surprise and anguish—

"Sacrilege!" Sir Harold wailed.

I rushed from my tent to find him hopping about in an excess of emotion. Everyone had gathered around, but no one cared to interrupt his rage. He was too excited to speak coherently for some time, an unusual state for a man who was normally calm and self-assured. Eventually he settled sufficiently to grasp my arm, and pointing toward the tent where the mummy was kept, he said, "Our mummy—our fine mummy—vandals—" He was grinding his teeth, pale with outrage. I walked over to the tent and looked in. It appeared that somehow during the night a vandal had indeed obtained access to our precious find. The sarcophagus was thrown open, and the mummy had been disturbed. A long gash had been made down the front of the torso, the linen wrappings were unpeeled, and the ancient flesh had been opened wide. The cut itself was clean, almost surgical, and the marcescent innards overflowed from the corpse like the sawdust from a rag doll, spilling in a dry cascade down the withered chest and into the sides of the sarcophagus. The corpse had been mummified too long for this to be disgusting, of course, but the act itself was shocking. I well understood Sir Harold's use of the word sacrilege and that his outburst was justified. The vandalism seemed pointless and incomprehensible.

Sir Harold spent the day in gloom, trying to discover who the culprit was and having no success. The damage itself was not irreparable, but the question remained, why should it have been inflicted? We discussed various possibilities. Certainly nothing had been gained by the act, and it seemed purely malicious. Finally we concluded that one of the workers, nursing a grievance against Sir Harold and knowing how enraged he would be by the vandalism, had done it expressly for spite. But we could conceive of no occurrence which might have given rise to the deed. Only one alternative suggested itself; namely that someone, resenting the disturbance of the ancient dead, had chosen this method to avenge the corpse. That did not seem likely, however, in that the mummy itself had been further defiled—hardly the means one would choose to manifest respect for one's ancestors. Only later did a third possibility occur to me. Thinking of Mallory and knowing him for an antagonistic man, I wondered if professional jealousy could have been responsible. I didn't really believe this, however, and did not choose to disclose my conjecture to anyone else.

In the end, it turned out all right for Sir Harold.

The newspapers fastened upon the vandalism and presented the story in rather sensational terms, hinting darkly of an ancient cult and of curses awaiting those who disturbed the dead. Sir Harold became more famous than ever. Perhaps that was as it should be. It was, after all, his expedition.

Although we persevered for another month at the site, no further noteworthy finds were unearthed. My translations served somewhat to explain this, confirming that our mummy had been a minor figure, a priest or physician—the names being interchangeable at the time, which showed how much their science and religion were interdependent—who had earned the pharaoh's favor to the degree that he was rewarded by mummification, but not to the extent that he merited an elaborate tomb. That, or possibly growing fear of grave robbers, explained why the sarcophagus had been uncovered, isolated, in the natural rock cliff and why there were few other finds in the immediate area. When I revealed this information to Sir Harold he decided there was little point in further work at the dig. He was not displeased. The publicity attending the vandalism had been greater than Sir Harold had enjoyed on any of his more successful expeditions, and he was entertaining pleasant expectations of his return to England. His strength was in retrospect; his value to his science was in public relations, and to give him credit, he undoubtedly realized that. Thus our work came to an end. We broke camp and returned to Cairo.

There was some delay in shipping our equipment and supplies, and we found it necessary to hold over in Cairo for several days. Sir Harold called a press conference, his agents arranged for the transport, and I welcomed this brief respite in what—at least by comparison to the camp—was civilization and decided to occupy several days as a tourist. It was during this period that I chanced to meet Mallory for the second time.

I had stopped rather late in the evening at one of those nightclubs that still retain a colonial atmosphere by the reverse method of being stylized as native. The waiters wore white jackets and red fez, and the tables were low, the surface tiled, arranged around all four walls. One sat upon cushions. In the depressed center of the room, exposed to view from all sides, the belly dancers gyrated with nubile torsos and bored faces. I was guided to a seat and ordered a drink. The room was heavily scented with smoldering fragrance and darkly illumined, so that at first I could see only the lissome oiled-copper dancers amid shadows. At length my eyes adjusted. Curious about the clientele, I glanced at the adjacent table. The man seated there wore Arab dress. I leaned out slightly to see beyond him and, as I did so, noticed his face. It was none other than Lucian Mallory.

I addressed him, more through my surprise than any desire to solicit conversation, and he turned in his peculiar fashion, his head rotating on the swivel of his spine; he recognized me and extended greeting in a cheerful manner. It was immediately apparent that he was rather the worse—or the better —for drink. There was a carafe of white liquid and two glasses before him. As he shifted position, I saw he was in the company of a woman.

For a startled instant, I believed her to be naked.

Then I saw she wore an exiguous outfit of silk and tassels, and understood her to be one of the dancers. Her face was veiled. She clung possessively to Mallory's arm and nuzzled at his ear.

Mallory saw my look, and laughed.

"You see, it is as I told you in the wilderness," he said. "I seek to know the dynamic flow of the land."

"Quite."

"Will you take a drink with me?"

"I've already ordered," I said, just as the waiter appeared with my Scotch. Mallory frowned without malice and gestured at his carafe, then snapped his fingers at the waiter.

"Arrack," he said. "How can you know the people when you cling to things foreign even in your drink?"

"I'm rather fond of Scotch."

"Arrack is the thing!"

I couldn't resist rejoining, "Arrack, yes. Derived from the Arabic *araq*. The word means 'sweat.'"

Mallory chuckled.

"I don't like it," his companion murmured petulantly. "Why do you not buy me champagne?"

"Later, my dear."

"Champagne is better."

"She gets a commission on all the champagne she drinks, you understand," Mallory said. "Somehow even Moslems manage to justify alcohol if a commission is involved."

"Yes, I am not allowed to drink," said the girl. "I do it only to please you."

"Tell me, Ashley. How did your work go?"

"Well enough. Nothing startling."

"No more mummies?"

"No. A curious thing happened, however. It occurred the night you were at the camp, in fact. You may have heard something of it?"

"Can't say I have."

"Our mummy was vandalized."

Mallory betrayed no surprise.

"Indeed?"

"Yes. It was cut open along the chest. Most peculiar. Not torn open, you know, but cut very neatly, almost surgically, as if someone had dissected it."

Mallory was intently regarding his drink. "Bit late for a postmortem, eh?"

"By several thousand years."

"Ever find out who did it?"

"No, we didn't."

"That certainly is remarkable. Are you sure you won't try some of this arrack? No? Well. I expect Sir Harold was quite cut up about it? The mummy, I mean?"

"At first."

"Ah well, it was only a mummy, eh?"

"What an astonishing thing to say."

He peered at me from the caverns.

"Oh, it was a particularly fine specimen. I didn't mean to disparage your find. But it was just another mummy like all the others already in museums. Just exactly like the others, I daresay."

There was an implication here which I didn't comprehend.

"The same preparation for the afterlife," he continued. "The usual methods of embalming?"

"Oh, yes. Of course."

Mallory hesitated; he seemed to be weighing his thoughts and gauging me at the same time. Then he leaned closer. I could smell the arrack on his breath.

"What would you say if I told you I'd discovered a mummy —dating from the fourth millennium—that had been embalmed in a different manner?"

"Different? In what way? I suppose the process did vary from age to age—"

"A completely different way," he interrupted.

"But tell me how."

"Suppose a mummy was found which hadn't been disemboweled before it was embalmed? Suppose, furthermore, that even the contents of the skull were intact?"

"You mean that the internal organs were preserved?"

"Precisely."

I digested this. It seemed an extraneous point at first, but then various possibilities began to occur. A new form of preparing the dead for the afterlife might have significant bearing on our understanding of the ancient religious beliefs as well as casting light on the practical knowledge possessed in the past.

"Let me get this straight," I said. "This corpse was opened, the internal structure preserved by embalming, and then closed up again before the flesh was treated?"

Mallory nodded.

"Are you telling me you've found a mummy like this?"

He shrugged.

"I'm not yet certain," he said evasively.

"It would have to be x-rayed, of course."

"Oh, there are more direct methods. One does not, after all, have x-ray equipment in the field."

"What do you mean by 'more direct methods'?"

"Why, one could always cut open the torso," he said, and he was smiling and staring directly at me. Then he repeated his shrug and turned back to the girl. She wheedled for champagne. Mallory took a long swallow of arrack. I thought of our own mummy and of Mallory's seemingly pointless visit to our camp; of the equally pointless mutilation of the mummy. It gave one pause for thought. But Mallory must have been pulling my leg. He was, after all, quite drunk.

I turned from him and watched a bronze belly revolve before my table.

Those were the sole occasions of my acquaintance with Lucian Mallory. Four years had passed. They were not eventful years. I was still employed by the museum, but since my presence was not often required in the buildings, I took a cottage at Wealdstone and found it convenient to do most of my work at home. And there it was, on a chill and stormy day, that Mallory's letter found me. The envelope felt cold and was smudged with damp from the postman's fingers. I turned it about in my hands, playing a guessing game with the contents and musing upon the strange man I had met in Egypt. I could conceive of no reason why he should have written. At length I tired of the game and opened the letter.

He wrote:

The Croft
Farriers Bar
Devonshire

My dear Mr. Ashley,

I am taking the liberty of addressing myself to you on a matter of mutual interest. I now have—have had for some time, but have only recently returned from the West Indies—in my possession several parchments and clay tablets of as yet indeterminate age, discovered in the necropolis at Tel-el-Mose. The hieroglyphs are similar to what we know as the standard symbols of the time, but in certain ways they seem to vary. I find myself unable to render a satisfactory translation. I am aware you are considered one of the nation's leading hieroglyphists—a fact, I fear, of which I wasn't aware when we first met—and feel it would prove to our mutual advantage if you were to examine these writings and, if possible, effect a translation.

For obvious reasons, I do not wish these valuable objects to leave my possession, nor do my present affairs enable me to bring them to you. Therefore it is my hope, when and if it proves convenient, that you may find the time to come to me.

Trusting you are well, sir, and awaiting your reply, I have the honor to be,

Your obedient servant,
Lucian Mallory

I arranged another log on the fire and scanned the message again. I read it several times. The letter seemed deliberately vague, and had I not known Mallory, I'd have assumed it a hoax or a mistake; possibly the work of a tourist who, duped into the purchase of a shard of pottery at a stall in Cairo, now hoped for a free evaluation of some worthless article fresh from the potter's wheel.

But Mallory, although certainly an amateur, was no common tourist.

At the very least I knew that he had been in the desert, and although he'd never made it clear what he hoped to discover, he had pursued his investigations with personal effort and despite inconvenience. Mallory's ideas, what little I knew of them, seemed misguided. That did not however preclude his discovering valuable results, as it were, by a tangent. It didn't matter at all what he was looking for. It was what he had found that was important. And it seemed just possible he'd made a discovery which, although probably unrelated to his theories, was nonetheless of interest. It was not a chance I wished to pass up. A man looking for a pink unicorn may find a rare mountain ox; his motivation does not diminish his findings. Thus, wondering where Farriers Bar was located and whether the museum could be persuaded to cover my expenses, I prepared to visit Lucian Mallory.

2

Burdened by the weight of my solitary suitcase, I stood alone on the wooden platform and watched the train which had carried me from London jolt into motion, inertia surging through the couplings. It was dark now. The platform was abandoned to isolation and to dust. I carried my suitcase into the station, a drab room with official green paint unpeeling on the benches. The interior, too, was deserted but for one official-looking fellow at the counter. He resembled a parrot in a Victorian cage. A sign proclaimed this Farriers Bar, and an electric clock hummed on the wall beside discolored schedules and a poster advertising a flower show. Apparently Mallory hadn't summoned the courtesy to attend my arrival. It seemed only common decency, after I'd made the journey at his request, and I felt a momentary annoyance. It faded quickly, however. I hadn't really expected the ritual of courtesy from Mallory; one rather expected the unexpected. He was not a man who clung to the traditional social formulas except as it pleased him or perhaps shocked others. I thought of the white linen and silver in the wilderness in relation to the Arabian robes and belly dancers in Cairo. Too, he must have known I'd be eager to examine his discovery, and perhaps he believed he was extending me a favor. He might well be. I was certainly curious and intrigued by his letter and, truth be known, by the man himself.

I shifted the suitcase to my left hand and approached the ticket seller and/or stationmaster. He looked up over rimless spectacles through the gilt bars.

"I wonder if you might help me?"

"Might."

"Would you know where Lucian Mallory lives?"

"Mallory? Mallory?"

I recited the return address on his letter.

"Oh, The Croft. Of course. That'll be old Peter Hammond's house. Been empty for years. Old Peter, he died some six or seven years ago, you know."

"I didn't know that," I admitted, for the sake of propriety.

"Well, it's a fact. Died. 'Course, he was old. Come to think of it, I'd heard someone moved in there. Mallory, you say? Don't know how he'll ever heat that place, come winter."

"Where is the house?"

"It'll be two, maybe three miles west of town."

"I'd expected to be met. I don't suppose there's a taxi here?"

"Not here at the station. Might be one about in the village. Probably not at this hour. There's an inn there, leastwise, and you can get a cab come morning."

"I see."

"Only a brisk walk to the village. If you're a brisk walker, that is. You just follow the path along over the bridge." He paused and squinted. "Maybe you'll not want to be walking, what with the madman prowling about?"

"Madman?"

"You've not heard?"

I shook my head.

"We've had us a horrible murder. Horrible. Murder most foul." He sounded like a parrot that has been taught headlines from Victorian newspapers. He obviously was delighted over the atrocity. "In all the papers it was. Not just the local paper but *The Times* and all. Couldn't have been in the local paper, come to think of it. That doesn't come out until the Friday, you see."

"I'm afraid I don't read the papers often."

"That so? Well now, I thought you'd be working for one of them. That just goes to show how mistaken a man can be, eh?" He peered at me suspiciously, as if thinking I were not above deceit.

"Whatever gave you that idea?"

"Deduction. We don't get many gentlemen stopping at Farriers Bar, so the minute I saw you I deduced you were either from Scotland Yard or Fleet Street. That narrowed the choice down, you see? Then I saw you didn't look like a policeman, so I figured you must be a newspaper fella. It's simple elimination." He looked smug. Then he frowned. "But you say you aren't a newspaperman, eh? You aren't a policeman?"

"I'm afraid not."

"There you are again. Just goes to show how a man can be mistaken in his deductions."

"It certainly does."

"Well, you just follow the path over the bridge, and you'll be in the village in no time at all. The Red Lion is the inn you'll want. Decent place. You'll be there before you know it. Maybe—" he glanced sharply at me, obviously annoyed that I wasn't a newspaperman. "Maybe, who knows?—you'll even be there before the madman finds out that you're walking about all alone." He considered this and nodded. "Yes, I think there's a fair chance you'll get to the inn before the horrible madman gets to you."

"I'm sure I shall."

"Not that I'm recommending it, you understand. I wouldn't want that on my conscience."

"You've done all you can."

"Right you are."

I smiled and headed for the door. I could feel his eyes at my back. He still was undecided whether I might be a newspaperman, but his doubts were understandable. No man likes to have his logic proved false.

In the distance a train was running along the darkened landscape. I wondered if it was the same train that had brought me, but with the land obscure and the perspective uncertain, I couldn't tell. It was evocative, a train in the night with yellow windows and passengers peering out. For them, the land was receding and they were stationary; their destinations closed on them and they had only to wait, while their lives were guided as carefully through time as the train was guided through space. The points of human affairs are predetermined; we make our flawed decisions to no avail, for the manifold tracks of life stretch to but one terminal. A man can be distressed by this certainty, or he can be consoled.

That is our only choice.

More immediately, I had no choice.

Morning would be time enough to call on Mallory, and I began walking toward the village. A few mellow lights were visible ahead, and I could imagine the rustic and unspoiled appearance of Farriers Bar, a hamlet disdained by time. I was not opposed to such a life, although time plays an integral part in my vocation, and thought I understood why Mallory would live in a provincial region. I recalled his desire to experience the past, not in retrospect, but as it had been; as if it were the present.

The path ran straight between hedgerows, then rose and humped its back into a wooden arch across a stream. As I approached this bridge I noticed a figure leaning against the railing. At regular intervals a pipe flared in his mouth, carving a slice of illumination along his face. My approach was sound-less on the path, and the man failed to notice me until my first hollow footfall fell on the wooden bridge. Then he sprang abruptly away from the rail, turning to confront me. The pipe dropped from his open mouth and bounced, scattering sparks. His startled move, so unexpected, caused me to react in a similar manner. I stumbled back a step, and we surveyed each other rather stupidly. I saw he was an old man, obviously frightened.

"I'm sorry. I didn't mean to startle you."

"Lord, sir, I thought you was the monster."

I blinked. It was bad enough to be mistaken for a news-paperman. The old man was bending over, looking for his pipe. I saw it balanced on the edge of the bridge and retrieved it for him. He nodded his thanks and peered into the black-ened bowl. It had gone out, but a few shreds of tobacco remained. He struck a match and sucked noisily until the pipe was burning to his satisfaction.

"Monster?" I said.

"I meant no offense, sir. It was the way you'd come upon me so suddenlike. I hadn't a good look at you in the dark. I didn't mean to imply you had the aspect of a monster, no sir. But you've not half given me a fright." He shook his head wryly. "It's bad enough having to keep on the hop when the constable's about, without having a monster to add to a man's troubles."

"Do you mean, this madman?"

"However it may be. Monster, to my way of thinking."

He nodded, his pipe inclining, to enforce his words. I won-dered just what connotation the word "monster" had to this rustic fellow, and inquired, "What sort of monster?"

"Why, a proper monster, sir. You know."

"What makes you think that?"

He drew his aging body proudly erect and removed the

pipe from his mouth before he replied. Then he said, "I found the body, sir."

I searched his face for a hint of amusement, knowing that these country chaps are not above a jest at a stranger's expense. He seemed absolutely serious. He said, "A gentleman he was, too, sir. Not the monster. The victim. It was plain he was a gentleman by his clothing, you see. What was left of his clothing. It was a terrible thing. The poor gentleman's arm was fair tore off, and his head was sort of flattened and unshaped. It gave a man a shock, I don't mind telling you, finding him like that."

He paused, as if waiting a request to continue. I must confess to interest in his tale and suppose most men are drawn to the sensational.

"How did you come to find the body?"

He looked at me openly and slyly at the same time, a not inconsiderable feat.

"I don't expect you'd be a policeman?" he asked.

"Neither monster nor minion of the law."

He chuckled.

"That's good, that is," he said. "I can see you've a way with words. I've been told I could use the King's English myself, although I've not had education. But you'd be interested in my story, would you?"

"I would."

"Well, sir, my name is Melville Coots, and I'm what is known as a poacher. That is a man what poaches. Now that is considered by the authorities to be contrary to the law of the land, but I don't hold with that. Wouldn't do it, if I did. For after all, we must have laws. But I just take a rabbit now and again. For the stewpot, you know. No harm in that. A man is entitled to get a crust however he can these days, what with taxes and government and immigrants and suchlike. My pension wouldn't hardly keep me in tobacco—"

Saying this, he looked into his pipe, then tapped the bowl

against his hand. I offered him my tobacco pouch, and he filled his pipe carefully, thumbing each layer down and stuffing in a considerable quantity. Then he leveled the top and lighted it again.

"Ah, that's good, that is," he said, his leathery old face wreathed in smoke. "Let's see now. Ah, yes. It was just the other night—I has to poach at night, see, so I don't have the misfortune to be apprehended by Constable Chive, who is constantly on the lookout during the day." The aged man's eyes assumed an attitude of fleeting indignation, but then he entered his narrative in earnest. "The other night I was setting my snares in the woodlands west of the village. It was a fine night with a bright moon so that the leaves were all silvery and the shadows like black cobwebs. I'd come into a little glade that looked fine for my purpose, as the rabbits are wont to romp in such places. I bent down to fix my snare. Suddenly, some instinct made me look up. And there he were, not three feet away from me, leaning against a tree. I didn't realize it were a dead man, at first. I stared at him, and he stared right back at me with one open eye. The other eye was all squished in. Well, when I saw this, I had my first inkling that all was not right. But I still didn't see that he was dead. I began to tremble. Then I got myself together and showed my electric torch on his face. Just as I did, as if the light itself had caused it, his mouth dropped open. Lord! It's a wonder I didn't have a stroke. I have never known a mouth to open so wide. It dropped right down so that his jaw rested on his breastbone, like he was planning to take a great bite out of my torchlight."

The old man shuddered slightly, as if reexperiencing the encounter, but then continued: "Well, I guess I ran then. I'm not ashamed to admit it. Don't really remember it, neither, except the next thing I knew I was some distance away, leaning against a tree and shaking. I still had the torch in my hand, and I was shaking so much that the whole woods was shimmering. Finally I calmed down somewhat. It came to me then that the poor gentleman meant me no harm and that, in fact, he was no longer living. Death, now, is a different matter. A man can't be scared of death, as it is the proper end of all things, except of course his own death which a man is entitled to be scared of, proper or not. So I told myself I was obliged to go back, and I did, sort of sneaking through the trees.

"I didn't go so close this time, but showed the torch on him from a distance. This gave me a more orderly advantage than I'd had with his mouth open right before my nose, and I could plainly see he was dead. His arm was hanging by a few tendons from his shoulder, and there was plenty of dried blood on him and on the ground. His jaw was broken—that's why it had opened so wide, you see, the hinges were cracked. I didn't go no closer. I took stock of the situation and figured I had to do my duty. Killing people isn't on the same order as poaching, and the laws against homicide are laws which I hold with. Venerable laws. And it was plain that someone had done for this poor gentleman, as his injuries were such as could not readily be caused by misadventure or accident. So it was clearly my duty to inform Constable Chive of this body in the woods. First though, being acquainted with Chive, I had to gather up the snares I'd already set and secret them. I didn't like to do that, but it isn't always convenient to do one's duty, so I did. I hid them in a little spot I know, the location of which I won't mention. Then I hurried into the village and sought out the constable."

Coots snorted.

"Lot of good it did me," he said.

"He didn't believe you?"

"Oh, I'm known as a man of my word, he believed me all right—once he allowed me to tell my tale. But at first he kept interrupting me. Wanted to know what I was about in the woodlands at that hour, you see. Asked all sorts of questions inferring I'd no business to be there. It was plain that he was more concerned with collaring me for poaching than seeking clues to a genuine crime." Coots shook his head in long-suffering resignation. "That's the way of policemen. They have an unfortunate habit of mistaking law for justice and spend more time intimidating honest citizens than deducing the nature of crimes. Ah, well.

"Finally I got through to him. He got all excited then. Never had a genuine murder to solve, old Chive. You could just see his face light up with thoughts of forensic glory and promotion. The Sherlock Holmes of Farriers Bar, that's what he was thinking. He had me take him out to the woods to see for himself, and it was a different matter then. Old Chive never saw such a thing in his life. Saw a handful of mangled corpses, I suppose, what with motorcar smashes and the like, but never a gory murder victim. Mind, I never saw such a thing before, neither. But it was different for me, being just a citizen. Chive had his duty to do. Just the sight of that corpse was enough to boil away all thoughts of glory. He sent for help straight off."

"That was quite an experience."

"It surely was."

"Have they any idea who the killer is?"

Coots shrugged.

"They never let on, do they, sir?"

"I suppose not."

"There's talk of a madman around the village, but I hold more to the monster theory. They've had an inspector come down to take charge of the investigation, and he asked me plenty of questions. Inspectors aren't the sort to trouble themselves about poachers, you see, so I didn't mind talking to him. But he didn't seem too keen on the monster theory. Got his own ideas. You'd think they'd show a little respect, though, seeing as how I found the body. I ought to know more about it than them, being in on the ground floor, so to speak. They just got no imagination, none of them policemen. Set in their ways. Once they catch a criminal they study him in detail, you see, and this fixes their way of thinking. The next time they're called on to pursue a criminal, they think he'll be just the same as the other one. That's why they never nabbed Jack the Ripper, to my way of thinking. I reckon Jack was a monster, too."

He leaned back against the rail, pensively puffing on his pipe.

"Probably lots more monsters lurking about than people give credit for."

"You're probably right," I said.

"'Course, they never do let on, do they? What I mean is, they got vice squads and homicide squads and suchlike, for all we know they got a monster squad, too. Only it's hushed up. They wouldn't want people to know about that. Might cause panic. Like when they don't tell you about epidemics and things that immigrants bring in. All them alien diseases and infestations. It's all kept secret. Politics." He shook his head gravely. "Do you believe in monsters, then, sir?"

"Well, truth is stranger than fiction," I conceded, choosing my words carefully.

"Nothing stranger than a monster, though."

I nodded solemnly.

We exchanged a few pleasantries, oddly inappropriate after his previous tale, and he told me it was a pleasure to discuss things with an open-minded man. Then I continued on toward the village. After I'd walked for fifty yards or so, I glanced back. Coots was still standing on the bridge, a slight dark shape. His pipe glowed with a pulsing rhythm, and he gave the impression of a man deep in thought, contemplating life as he knew it. I walked on into Farriers Bar.

I passed several cottages with thatched roofs and quite suddenly found myself in the center of the village. It seemed a prototype of its kind. The street was cobbled, the footpath narrow, and although lanes issued off the high street, the village gave the impression of being linear, without depth. All the shops were closed, and there was a splendid little church. There were no automobiles to be seen. A policeman was walking slowly down the opposite side of the street, his high helmeted shadow on the walls. I assumed this was Coots's nemesis, Constable Chive. As he drew opposite, he glanced across the narrow road, and I saw an indistinct pale face. His steps slowed, and I half expected him to cross over and interrogate me. Having already, within half an hour, been mistaken for a newspaperman and a monster, I was mildly paranoid and, for all I knew, could be taken for a poacher as well. But he walked on, and so did I. A moment later I came to the Red Lion.

It was an agreeable surprise.

In times past, Farriers Bar must have been a stopping point on a route from somewhere to another, for the Red Lion was a fine old coaching inn built around an open archway through which a coach could be driven and the horses stabled in the interior courtyard. It had been only slightly modernized. The hotel entrance was on one side of the arch, the public house on the other. Antique lanterns were set on either side of the doors, and although they used electricity now, the incandescence was mellowed by golden glass.

I entered through the hotel doorway and stopped at the desk. There was a bell which I pressed, and a few minutes later a buxom blonde woman, not yet old, appeared from a side door. She wore an old-fashioned lace collar and rather more cosmetics than seemed suitable for a venerable inn. She was friendly and smiled as she moved behind the desk.

"Do you have a room?" I asked.

"Got twelve of 'em, matter of fact."

"One should do me."

"Single?"

She looked as if she were inquiring about my marital status, but I assumed she meant the room and nodded. Then she said, "Bath?" as if she wondered whether I did. I agreed.

She pushed the register across, an antient tome with a leather cover, opened toward the final page.

"Mabel Sinclair," she said. "I own this place. Been behind the bar, sorry to keep you waiting."

"Quite all right."

I signed the register. She turned the book around and studied my signature.

"Will you be staying long, Mr. Ashley?"

"Just overnight. Possibly tomorrow."

"You can park your car in the courtyard."

"I haven't a car."

"That so?"

"I came on the train."

"Well, isn't that something?"

I agreed it was something.

She had removed a key from the board and placed it on the desk but kept her hand over it.

"Don't get many folks on the train these days. Don't get many folks coming to Farriers Bar by any means, matter of fact." She had a brassy, but pleasant laugh. "Will you be requiring dinner?"

"I think not. A sandwich, perhaps."

"You can get a sandwich in the bar. Just the other side of the arch. Don't have to worry about closin' time, long as you come in the side door. That shows you're registered as a guest; what's called a bona fide traveler. Handy law, that. Open to abuse, though. We get the odd gentleman who registers and pays for a room just so he can drink after time. Sometimes they don't even make use of the room. That's why I have to insist they pay in advance—"

She smiled apologetically with lipstick on her teeth.

"Quite understandable," I said.

I offered money. She took it with the same hand that had concealed the key, thereby relinquishing it without emphasizing the exchange. The key was attached to a large brass ball so that a guest wouldn't forget it was in his pocket.

"Up the stairs, second on the right." She motioned toward the staircase. "Or should I show you up?"

"I'll find it, thank you."

"Sorry there isn't a porter. 'Fraid we don't do much business here. I'll be in the pub, you need anything."

I thanked her once more, she retreated through the side door, and I carried my bag up the wide staircase and down the hall. My room was labeled with brass numbers, and several attempts were required before I correctly fitted the key into the lock. The door creaked. The room was large with a high paneled ceiling and a tall window overlooking the high street. The bed was huge and soft, covered with a rose-colored quilt. On the wall beside the door, slightly askew, was an oil painting of indifferent quality and ingenious geography, depicting the monoliths of Stonehenge rising above a stormy sea. I thought it likely this original work of art had been commissioned in payment for room and board at some past time when payment was not required in advance.

I felt a touch of sympathy for the unknown artist and straightened the painting so that it squared with the walls, which were none too symmetrical themselves. It still didn't look right. I decided that the painting, whatever its aesthetic qualities, was at least obedient to physical laws and acted as a plumb line, dutiful to gravity rather than to architecture. I pushed it back where it had been, then opened my valise and hung my suit in the closet. The suit depended at precisely the same angle as the painting, which seemed to prove my plumbline theory. This was gratifying; I realized how the unknown ancient builder must have felt when he created the first plumb rule and determined the perpendicular in the construction of the pyramids. The builders of Stonehenge, too, must have known this physical law, and it pleased me to think that the painting, because of its subject, manifested the same principle. The variance between wall and painting, however, was almost alarming, and it was evident that this building would fall long before the great slabs of Stonehenge or the monstrous wedges of the desert. This was a fact which, I reflected wryly, Lucian Mallory could work nicely into his concept of the past: the lost skills and sciences of the ancients; the notion of time as a fluid constant in which events were congealed like lumps of fruit in aspic. I felt a sense of eternity fall over me with these thoughts, and outside the window Constable Chive passed once more, in the other direction, his hollow footfalls resounding as punctuation in the passage of time.

In this philosophic mood, I went back down the stairs and through the side door. This placed me under the arch, and I paused there, fancifully listening for a clatter of hooves and a rattle of wheels. For a moment I could have sworn I heard those anachronistic sounds. Once, deep within the Great Pyramid, I had perceived the labored groans of ten thousand slaves and the tormented cries of the grave robbers as the ancient traps worked, burying them under tons of sand. I had heard them distinctly, those echoes of eternity that had existed thousands of years before, as if the vibrations had been trapped in the very stones and, from time to time, had seeped out. It had excited me. It had frightened me. Could the sounds of great stress and unspeakable torment be congealed in the walls? Could a place be haunted by lithic possession? Could emotion be so powerful that the very molecules of the naked rock were altered? If time were truly constant, could not the dimensions of our existence overlap? I had been alone in the pyramid, the sounds had subsided and faded into silence, but I have never doubted that I heard them, not within my imagination, but as physical waves.

And for a moment as I stood under the arch, the same phenomenon occurred. The rumble of a horse-drawn carriage echoed up the articulation of my spine. I turned toward the entrance, startled. There was nothing there. No steed appeared with wide white eyes and foaming teeth; no elegant brougham with liveried attendants encroached upon my consciousness. The sound had receded in an instant. I looked back at the courtyard. Only a bicycle was stabled there, chained to the watering trough. I smiled at myself, but my backbone still tingled. I went through the opposite door and into the bar.

3

The bar was medieval, an oblong room with a low ceiling crossed by heavy blackened beams and several stout tables of aged oak. A polished brass rail extended the length of the bar just above the floor, and a sequence of pewter mugs hung down over it. A most agreeable room. Unfortunately, an American-style jukebox squatted in the corner, bubbling with gay purple lights. It was not playing at the moment, but there it lurked, threatening a cacophonous onslaught at any instant. I eyed it dubiously. There are few things as minatory as a jukebox in a public house, in the scheme of mechanical menace. I rated it just behind a telephone in a secluded cottage and just ahead of an empty typewriter on a desk when one's work is being neglected. I approached the bar and positioned myself so that the damned thing could not attack me from the rear. Mabel Sinclair moved to serve me, preceded by her lipsticked smile. I asked for a sandwich and a pint of bitter. The beer was excellent, the sandwich unidentifiable. Mabel noticed the way I regarded her jukebox.

"Pretty modern, eh?" she said.

"It is that, yes."

"Only jukebox in the whole village."

"I'm sure."

"Fella from the vending machine company kept after me for a whole year to put it in, you know. I wasn't sure how it would fit in with the what you call decor. What do you think?"

"Well, as you say, it's modern."

"That's so. Some of the old-time customers weren't too keen on havin' it here. On the other hand, lots of the young folks in the village like it. Trouble is, most of them as likes it are too young to come into the bar. I ain't too sure about it, myself. Got some good records, though. Got some Tom Jones records."

"Is that so?"

"Oh, yes. Three or four of them. You like Tom Jones?"

"He was a fine miner."

Mabel squinted.

"He's bloody awful," said one of the sterling chaps at the dart board.

Mabel scowled at him.

"Old-fashioned," she told me.

He grunted and threw for double tops. He missed.

Mabel said, "I like to keep up with the times, myself. I figure a girl has to keep herself abreast of the times, don't you? I mean, this ain't the Victorian Age. People are broad-minded now. Mind you, I've always been a broad-minded old sort. You can ask any of the locals, they'll tell you I don't give tuppence for what anyone does. Long as they don't cause trouble here in the pub, that is. Otherwise I'd have Chive on my neck. Chive's the village constable. He's a right stickler for the law, is Chive. 'Course, that's his job. But I figure he's just envious 'cause he can't drink while he's on duty."

"I've heard about Constable Chive."

"That so?"

"Mr. Coots mentioned him."

"Coots? You a friend of old Coots?"

"Not really. I just met him as I was walking from the station."

"Hah. Out poachin', I'll wager. He's a right old rogue, is Coots. Listen, I'll tell you something about Coots. Ah—where you from?"

"London."

She nodded, verifying my statement.

"Yes, well, seein' as you're from London, you'll not be shocked to hear this, so I don't mind tellin' you. Old Coots has propositioned me. Fancy that! Me! Don't know whatever possessed the old boy—"

"He must be daft," said the old-fashioned dart player.

Mabel shot him a wicked glance.

I was trying to think of a way to change the subject, but Mabel continued, "'Course there are those that consider me attractive. Not just old Coots. Lots of men. You'd be surprised if I told you. Married men, even. Not that I'd reveal their names. That wouldn't be right, you'll just have to take my word for it."

"I certainly do."

"You see, I'm a widow. A gay widow, ha ha. My husband passed on a few years ago. Retired naval type, lots older than me. Don't know why I married him. This was his inn. Say, ha ha, maybe that's why I married him." She shook her head. "No, I shouldn't speak that way about the dead. Anyhow, he was a stuffy old sod, didn't like a bit of fun. Didn't even care to have what you call marital relations more than once a month or so. Mind you, I treated him right. I was a good wife to him. The way I figure it, if you're going to wed a bloke, you're entitled to treat him right. I didn't play around on him. Leastways, not much. Not what you'd call blatant. But then he passed on, rest his soul, and left this inn to me." Mabel paused a moment, as though in observance of silent obsequies for her departed husband, but then abruptly resumed her recital. "Well, I looked at myself after the funeral—looked right in the looking glass, you know—just as if I was looking at someone else, takin' stock of the situation. And I said, Mabel, old gel, you're still young and you've still got your looks and you're a woman of property now, and there's no reason why you shouldn't have some fun now you're unattached. That's just what I said, right out loud. Now, some folks might think that was the wrong sentiment to have, with the old boy hardly cold in the grave, but the way I see it, once he was dead and gone, why, what the hell! I'll be cold in my own grave soon enough. So I don't see how it was much of a sin."

She looked at me with raised eyebrows.

"You' re quite right."

She smiled and leaned closer. She was truly buxom and blossomed across the bar, threatening to envelop my pint. I withdrew it hastily. The dart player exclaimed cheerfully as he finally doubled out. The jukebox bubbled. We'll all be cold in our graves soon enough, I thought, just like eighty billion of our evolutionary ancestors, and I couldn't castigate this lively woman for whatever method she chose to impress some significance upon her passing years.

"Let's have another pint," I said.

"Fancy you meeting Coots," Mabel muttered, as she pulled it.

This was an opportune moment to change the subject, and I said, "He tells me he discovered a murder victim recently."

"He certainly did."

She placed the mug before me, the barm overflowing onto the quercine counter.

"Old Coots is right chuffed with himself, makin' a discovery like that. Why, if it weren't for him, the body might never have been found. Just goes to show, there's somethin' to be said for poachin'. Most excitement we've ever had in the village, I reckon, what with policemen and newspaper fellas and the like. 'Course, it wasn't a local gentleman, so the village can enjoy the excitement without havin' to mourn. Not that we wish harm to any strangers."

"They've not identified the body?"

"Not as far as I know."

"Yes, I can see how it would cause excitement in a peaceful little village like this."

"Only murder we've ever had here."

The dart players had come to the bar for refills. The old-fashioned one said, "No, there was a murder here in 1897. You ain't forgettin' that, Mabel?"

"Well, that might have been an accident—"

"Accident? You just don't want to give the Red Lion a bad reputation. It was murder right enough."

"Double murder, it was," the second player added. "Right here at the inn."

Mabel turned to me.

"Never was proved as murder," she explained.

"What happened?" I asked.

"Well, it was like this. The wife of the squire was having an affair with a local lad—"

"Blacksmith's son," the dart player said.

"That's right. Very sordid. She'd been meeting him for almost a year. About once a week. I read a book about it once. Well, sometimes they went to the blacksmith's shop and sometimes they took a room here at the Red Lion. I guess the innkeeper in those days was sort of broad-minded. Well, one fine day the squire came to hear of it. According to this book I read, the squire was a short-tempered bloke, and when he found out his lady was unfaithful he flew into a proper rage. Can't say as he can be blamed. He had his carriage hitched up to a fine pair of horses, jet black they were with fiery eyes. The stable lad explained about that at the inquest. Said that the master's eyes were burnin' just like the horses', blazin' away like to frighten the devil. So off to town he comes, fixin' to catch his lady in the act.

"Well, sir, the lady and her lover were taking drink in the bar —right here at this very same bar, you see—and gettin' themselves ready to repair to the room they had already arranged for. As chance would have it—according to this book—they were just coming out of the public house, arm in arm and in their cups, as the squire turned his horses into the archway. He saw them at the same instant they saw him. His wife screamed and her lover threw up his hands and the squire started to rein in his horses with a terrible clatter, howling like a fiend. And then, quick as a flash, a terrible look came over his face. He let the reins go and whipped the horses savagely. They leaped forward onto the cobblestones and thundered directly over the lady and her lover.

"The blacksmith's son tried to protect his mistress by throwing himself over her, and the horses passed over them, but the heavy carriage rolled on and crushed them both under the churning wheels with the squire whippin' away at the horses the whole time. You could hear the both of them screaming all the way to the bridge, so this book said. They were lying there all crushed together, holding each other like lovers except that their insides had skidded out along the stones and they were all jellied. It was an awful sight. The squire jumped from his carriage and rushed back to the arch. He stood over them with his face all white and his eyes black and his hands clenched at his sides. His wife looked up at him and tried to speak, but only a death rattle came out. The squire didn't say a word. He waited until she was dead—although the blacksmith's lad was still twitching—and then he walked back to where the horses had come to a halt by the stables. They were snorting nervously and pawing the ground, their flanks white with froth. The squire drew a revolver from his pocket and very deliberately shot the horses in the head, one after the other. They fell dead on the spot, their corpses steaming. The squire threw his gun down and sank to his knees, pressing both hands to his face and uttering horrible curses.

"Well, there was an inquest, of course, and the verdict was that it had been an accident. None of the locals believed that, though. The squire was a cunning old bugger, you see, and it had been a stroke of genius, shootin' the horses the way he did, as if it had been the poor dumb brutes who were responsible. That carried a lot of weight at the inquest. They were very valuable horses, you see. And no one thought to ask why the squire had his gun with him at the time."

I was staring at her.

"You all right?" she asked.

I nodded.

"Why, I had no intention of upsetting your stomach with such a story, Mr. Ashley," Mabel said. But there was nothing wrong with my stomach; it was my mind that shivered and my flesh that turned cold as I remembered the sounds which had echoed under that very arch. I managed to affect a smile and took a long swig of beer. It fell violently into my belly as if cascading into a void.

Wonder does not demand thoughtless belief in the supernatural, and the supernatural becomes natural with knowledge. As Mallory had said, what was magic to the past is science to us, and by projection, what seemed magic to me now could be science in some distant future. Nevertheless, the chill of the unknown was not dissipated by a rational attitude. I reasoned that the sounds I had heard under the arch—and in the pyramid, for that matter—must have some explanation within the laws of the universe; yet, knowing this, the limitations of the language of thought still held me captive—I knew, despite reason, that I had heard a ghostly sound. Perhaps some abnormality in my aural structure was responsible; perhaps my ears were somehow attuned to the wavelengths of the past and could draw them out from where they still faintly trembled at the very core of the naked stone. Or, if Mallory were right, I may have experienced the simultaneous transmissions of another dimension, parallel to my own within eternity. I considered these possibilities in a rather vague fashion, sitting at the medieval bar and feeling links with the past even as the jukebox bubbled through the present and the dart players chatted with the barmaid. The clock moved slowly on, registering time as we experienced it.

Presently, through the side door, a man entered. I glanced at him, then looked closer. I believed that I knew him. He stood beside me at the bar and asked for a brandy, and at the sound of his voice, recognition dropped into place.

"John Cunningham!" I exclaimed.

He turned toward me. His face had become hardened and thinned, and his shoulders were stooped as if under a burden. But I'd not seen him in years, since before I'd been in Egypt, and such changes are natural with age.

"Ashley?"

We shook hands.

"What are you doing in this godforsaken place?" he asked.

Mabel placed his brandy before him and sniffed.

"Godforsaken, indeed," she said.

"Sorry, Mabel."

"Plenty of God around here," she added. "It's the cities that are godforsaken. Where they got all them immoral youngsters and immigrants and criminals. 'Course, we had a murder here, but I'll wager the killer comes from the city. That's plain, nobody around here is a killer."

"I daresay you're right."

"I'm stopping here for a day or two," I explained. "I've some business to attend to. But I might ask you the same thing."

"Oh, I'm living here," John said.

"In Farriers Bar?"

"Right here at the Red Lion, in fact."

"How remarkable. I thought your house—"

"Oh, I've closed up the house, Ashley. It was—" he paused, then said, "The house was too big, living alone." He acknowledged this as though nibbling at the perimeter of fact.

"Is Arabella married then?"

John was regarding his brandy contemplatively, as if seeking the answer to my query in the reflecting amber. He took a drink and winced. Whatever reflection he'd seen there continued to radiate in his stomach.

"No, she's gone elsewhere," he stated quietly.

"I suppose she's quite grown up now," I said, realizing

this wasn't a point to be pressed. I had remembered John as a cheerful, outgoing sort, rather older than I but retaining a youthful vigor. No more. Something more tragic than age seemed to have altered him to a depth more basic than appearance. Arabella was a lovely girl—a fine young woman by this time, I guessed—and John had cared for her greatly. His wife had died when Arabella was a mere child, and John had raised the girl on his own, his life directed by the process.

"Yes, they all grow up, don't they," he said.

"Well, it' s good to see you again."

He nodded absently. His glass was empty, and he turned it about in his hands for a moment, then pushed it across the bar and raised his eyebrows. Mabel frowned.

"You know what Dr. Plum told you," she said.

John looked pained.

"Why don't you have a nice pint of beer instead?"

"Mabel, be a good girl and give me a brandy."

"Well, I'm sure it's not my concern, you care to drink yourself to an early grave."

John winked at me.

"Mabel worries about her lodgers," he said. "Can't say if she's concerned with my health or my custom, though."

Mabel snorted and refilled his glass with a shrug, then said, "Rots the brain, brandy does. It's the grape, you know. A bit of the malt or the grain does no harm, but the grape is wicked poison. They say that's what's wrong with the Frenchies. All that grape."

"Who says that?"

"Well, they all say that."

"Oh."

A telephone rang faintly in the background. I was pleased to note that the phone wasn't in the bar, for in combination with the jukebox it would have been formidable. Mabel moved down the bar but turned back to say, "It causes the body to rot, that brandy. It gets right into the tissues. A man as drinks too much brandy has already started to waste into corruption even while he's still alive. You might as well drink embalming fluid and have done with it." She went out, shaking her head. John smiled after her.

"A kindly woman," he said.

"Have you really been drinking too much?" I asked, quite aware it was none of my business.

"Ah, the local doctor is as insular as Mabel. It's not the drink. They're simply suspicious of foreign tinctures. He wouldn't object to Scotch."

"Tinctures? You make it sound like medicine."

John smiled.

"Venerable medicine," he said. "Man relied on the grape long before miracle drugs." He shrugged. "You're a student of the past, Ashley. Who first ate some rotting fruit and discovered the benefits of alcohol? What worthy ancestor of man suffered the initial hangover?"

"I'm afraid that event long preceded anything open to my translations."

"And will terminate long beyond, eh? When the weird descendants of man have forsaken language and communicate by mathematical symbols? Or longer yet. When the next inheritors of the earth—what, the cockroach? the dragon fly?—discover the arts of fermentation and zymurgy? Which will last longest, Ashley, religion or alcohol?" He downed his drink. "Granted both are bores, give me the drunkard over the zealot."

Before I could reply, Mabel Sinclair returned. She was obviously distraught. Her face had paled under its generous layer of powder, and her eyes flicked nervously about. It was evident the telephone call had shaken her. She poured herself a large whiskey and took a sip, coughed and drank again. Then she leaned across the bar and, in a hushed voice, said, "They've found another dead one."

The dart players gathered around, eager for the news, and Mabel cleared her throat. She looked at each of her customers in turn, determined that she held all interest, and announced, "That was Emma on the phone. Emma is the postmistress," she told me. "She's a terrible gossip and is calling everyone on the line so as to be first with the dreadful news. Can't say I blame her, in this instance, for she feels her responsibility. She's all cut up over it."

"How's that?" John asked.

"Why, it was the Brooke lad, you see. Little Raymond Brooke. Not hardly more than seventeen he was. Such a terrible thing. It was awful enough when they killed that city bloke, but why would anyone want to harm little Raymond. You must have known him, Mr. Cunningham?"

"I believe I've seen him about."

"His father is the tobacconist down the corner."

"Yes, of course."

"And he was so pleased with his new bicycle, too. That makes it all the worse. Why, I remember his father gave it to him on his birthday, must be two, three months ago now. Must have been his seventeenth birthday, I reckon."

"What has the bicycle to do with it?" John inquired. "Was it an accident?"

"Accident! Not likely. It was murder, right enough."

"But the bicycle?"

"And why should the postmistress feel responsible?" I asked.

"Why, he was the messenger for the post office, don't you see? Emma had sent him out to deliver a telegram yesterday afternoon. Well, he never came home that night and they've been looking for him and they just found his poor little body beside the road. It must have happened while he was bicycling out with the telegram. They say he was all broken up like the other fellow. Emma said he was all crushed up together with his bicycle, so that you couldn't even separate the two. They had to haul the body and the bike in together, and the doctor will have to cut them apart. Or maybe they'll just bury them together, I wouldn't know about that. He was so proud of his new bike. It was green. British racing green, he said."

"That sounds rather as if it were an accident," John muttered. "Some hit-and-run driver. If the body was mangled that much and found beside the road—"

Mabel shook her head vigorously.

"No. It was the madman, no doubt of that. The authorities have ways of knowing such things."

"The authorities, perhaps. But Emma—"

"Well, a postmistress is an authority, sort of."

An unpleasant idea already had occurred to me, for I didn't suppose there were a great many telegrams directed to Farriers Bar. Mabel was looking at everyone in rotation. When she turned to me, I asked, "I don't expect she told you to whom the telegram was sent?"

"Matter of fact, she did. That was an important point, you see. Wouldn't have happened if the telegram had been for someone in the village, so quite naturally she told me. It was addressed to the new resident out at The Croft. That's the old Hammond place—"

"My God," I said.

"What's the matter, Ashley?" John asked.

"I sent that telegram!"

John looked sharply at me, frowning slowly.

"What a dreadful sensation," I said. "It makes me feel, well, indirectly responsible."

"Just like Emma," Mabel said. "Maybe even more than Emma. Not that I hold you responsible, I don't mean that, but Emma didn't really have a choice. It was her official duty to send the telegram on once it arrived. But you didn't really have to send it in the first place, did you? I'm not blaming you, understand, but I can see how a man would blame himself."

"Why on earth were you sending a telegram to Mallory?" John asked me.

"You know him?"

With his teeth clenched, he said, "I know the man."

"It was a matter of some hieroglyphs he wished translated. I'd wondered why he hadn't met me at the station. Now it seems he never received my wire."

"And little Raymond is dead," Mabel added.

"Mallory is a scoundrel," John said.

I raised my eyebrows.

"You can hardly blame this on him."

"No, no. I didn't mean that. But you'd be wise to have nothing to do with him."

"I don't understand."

Mabel was staring at John with sympathy. He glanced at her, and she quickly averted an embarrassed expression. John grimaced and hunched over the bar. Over the chiming of the clock Mabel announced, "Time, gentlemen," nodding at the dart players. "Drink up before Chive comes poking around." They tipped back their glasses as the front door opened and a heavy-set man with an official demeanor came in, stamping loudly. Mabel took the empty glasses from the dart players, glancing at the clock. The dart players were regarding the intruder with that wonted apprehension which honest men reserve for the authorities. They began putting on their coats. The newcomer approached the bar, and Mabel gestured toward me and John.

"These gentlemen are registered here," she said.

He grunted curtly, without interest.

"Cunningham?"

John nodded.

"I'm Inspector Peal."

"I know who you are."

"I'd like to ask you a few questions, sir."

John did not reply. Mabel was busily washing glasses. The dart players departed, staring back over their shoulders. Mabel crossed the room and drew the bolt on the front door. She unplugged the jukebox, and the purple lights stopped bubbling with a strangled gurgle. She switched out the exterior and the overhead lights, closing up very thoroughly in deference to the inspector, who couldn't have cared less about licensing laws. The room darkened, illuminated only from behind the bar in long shadowed cones of light. I had the impression that our chamber had suddenly been catapulted back into the Middle Ages; that the inspector represented the Inquisition. Perhaps these are natural attitudes for an innocent citizen confronted by the presence of the law, for just as descriptive laws are excepted by magic, so are ordained laws invested by execution. Then Peal relaxed. His taut face loosened, and he sighed as he settled onto a stool. He was merely human, then, and rather weary, a man performing an unpleasant job.

John waited for him to speak.

Peal was seated obliquely to the bar, one elbow on the surface, so that only half his face was discernible. Some interplay of light and position made this a perfect bisection, the division running straight down his brow and the bridge of his nose and cutting his wide chin. It made him seem a figure playing dual roles—man and policeman, perhaps—but I wasn't sure which side was which. John was between us, facing the light but with his head down so that he too was divided, but laterally, an incandescent forehead shading a dark jaw. He presented a sullen appearance. Peal was gazing at me, past John, but registered no particular interest in my presence. It suddenly dawned on me that he was embarrassed; that he looked at me to avoid confronting John. For a confusing moment I actually thought the inspector had come to arrest John for the murders. But that was absurd. Strange circumstances stamp remarkable patterns on the mind.

"Perhaps I'd better leave," I suggested.

I made to depart. Peal didn't seem interested one way or the other, but John touched my arm.

"No, stay, Ashley."

I raised my eyebrows at Peal, and he granted permission with a nod.

"The inspector will probably want to interview you, too," John said. He looked at Peal. "I assume you're making the rounds of all the strangers and new residents?"

"That's right, sir. Just routine, you understand."

"I have an alibi, I'm afraid," said John, smiling faintly.

"I'm sure."

"But I suppose you'll be wondering why I decided to move here? Something of that nature?"

"I believe I already know that, sir," Peal replied. I sensed a disturbing undercurrent running between them; a significance deeper than the words. "I've already made inquiries about that." He turned to me and, as if to lessen the weight of the circumstances, added, "I'll probably be checking on you, too, sir. As I said, it's a matter of routine."

"Of course."

"Get on with it then," John said.

"Well, sir. I assume you moved here to be near your daughter?" Peal stated this hesitantly, almost delicately. John glanced at me, then nodded. Peal continued, "I was wondering, sir, if you could tell me anything about Mr. Mallory?"

"Mallory?" I said, speaking from surprise.

"I'm afraid, Ashley, that my daughter has gone to live with the man," John said. "Now you see why I call him a scoundrel. But no, Inspector, I know nothing about him."

"Nothing? Being as how your daughter is stopping at Mr. Mallory's, I thought—anything at all, you know, even if it seems irrelevant. We've come to rather a dead end there. No one seems to know anything about him."

"Why not ask my daughter?"

"Well, I did, actually, sir. She wasn't very helpful. Seemed, well, distracted. I wondered if perhaps she wasn't well?"

"Perhaps not."

"And, of course, it's no good asking a man about himself," Peal said, as if revealing forensic secrets.

"I can't help you."

"Surely your daughter has mentioned something?"

"My daughter, Inspector, did not even tell me she was going there. I don't see her these days."

"Yet you moved to the village—"

"To no avail."

"Um. You didn't see fit, under the circumstances, to have him investigated?"

"If you can't trace his background, Inspector, how in blazes do you suppose I could?"

"Yes, I see—"

"This is rather unpleasant for me, Inspector. If you have any specific questions?"

Peal withdrew a notebook from his breast pocket and flipped it open, apparently to secure a moment for silent deliberation. John looked at me. I felt uncomfortable. I was remembering Lucian Mallory in Cairo, drinking heavily, in the company of a half-naked belly dancer. I had no doubt that Mallory was a man of depraved appetites and that he certainly had no business with a girl like Arabella Cunningham. But Mallory wouldn't give a damn what effect he had on the lives of others. I recalled the awe with which his servant, Sam Cooper, had spoken of his intellect. If he were capable of making a disciple of a hard-bitten old soldier like Cooper, how easily could he charm and overwhelm an innocent girl. I remembered his deep eyes and had a vision of Arabella peering into those depths, helpless to resist his basest whim. John was staring at my face, as if he had an inkling of the thoughts which disturbed me. That would never do, and I turned away, not wishing to compound his grief. He said he knew nothing of Mallory, and it was far better that way. Undoubtedly he had imagined the worst, but had he known Mallory—

"Mabel! Give us a drink," John cried.

That worthy woman, who had been following the conversation under the guise of washing glasses, jumped at his command. She hastened to fetch the brandy bottle and proclaimed, "Mr. Cunningham is a registered guest, you know, Inspector. Registered right in the book." She filled John's glass, then looked at me. I shook my head. "Inspector?" she asked.

"No," he responded automatically. Then he said, "Wait, yes, maybe I will. A small whiskey." Mabel appeared amazed, certain this was a violation of ethics. She poured him a Scotch. He put away the notebook and took up the glass. Somehow his gesture of drinking manifested the difficulties he felt, the frustration of this investigation. He drained the whiskey in one swallow while John was sipping at his brandy.

"Just one more question, sir," Peal said. "Would you know if Mallory is a doctor?"

"A doctor?"

"Yes, a medical man."

"I shouldn't think so."

Peal frowned.

"Does he claim to be?" John inquired.

"Well, no. It was just an idea I had."

I felt it was time to speak up: "Perhaps I can help you, Inspector."

"And who might you be, sir?"

"Thomas Ashley."

His face went blank for a moment, then seemed to expand with interest. His brow arched and his lips tightened.

"Ashley—" he repeated.

"Yes, that's right. I sent the telegram."

"I see." He frowned. "How did you happen to know about that, then?"

"What?"

"The fact that the telegram was—never delivered."

"Why—"

"I told him, Inspector," Mabel said, looking up from the

sparkling glass she was cleansing for the fifth time. Then she blushed, realizing she had revealed her eavesdropping. "Emma phoned from the post office."

Peal snorted and shook his head.

"It figures," he grunted. "You'd think this was a bloody circus come to town." His words, like his drinking, betrayed his travail.

"You're acquainted with Mr. Mallory, then?"

"Very slightly."

"Your telegram stated you were arriving here. I assume you've come to see him?"

"Yes. He has some Egyptian hieroglyphs I'm interested in translating. Nothing to do with these murders, I assure you."

"Yes, yes," Peal nodded impatiently. "But do you know him?"

"I met him twice. In Egypt."

"Would you know what he does?"

"If you mean, is he a doctor—"

Peal gestured, turning a palm up.

"He's an Egyptologist," I affirmed. "At least, he was when I met him. He did mention having some medical background, but I shouldn't think he was a doctor. I'm sure he isn't."

"I see. An Egyptologist. He studies ancient ruins, things like that?"

"Things like that."

"So he told me."

"I see no reason to doubt him."

"Oh, I don't. We have to ask, that's all."

"Surely Mallory isn't a suspect?"

"Not at all. He's simply a new resident, and as I said, I'm naturally interested in anyone recently arrived here." He had produced the notebook once again. "If you'd just tell me anything you know about him—"

I hesitated. I had no liking for Mallory, yet on the other hand it seemed wrong to discuss him behind his back. Peal sensed my reluctance and commented dryly, "Curious, how people—especially innocent people—are so unwilling to talk to the authorities. Makes them feel like spies, eh? Damn silly attitude. If a man is innocent, what they say can only help prove it. And if he's guilty—I'm not talking about Mr. Mallory, you understand, just people in general—if a man is guilty, well, you'd think the citizens would be thankful to have him apprehended. But no. People seem to feel closer to criminals than to cops. It's as if the citizens, good and bad, are all allied against the laws; as if people want to lead their lives and policemen have to stop them. Almost part of the balance of nature."

"Is that a lecture?" I asked.

Peal looked at me.

"Laws, too, are good and bad," I said.

"I'm afraid so. No matter. I can't believe anyone would want to protect this killer. It's a grim thing, Mr. Ashley. They're always hard when there's no apparent motive, when it's the work of a madman. Oh, the madman thinks he has a motive, but how do you put yourself inside a twisted mind? There's no way to deduce who it is. You just have to look for concrete clues. And if he leaves no clues," Peal shrugged his shoulders, "well, then, you just have to wait and maybe you'll catch him in the act. Maybe you won't. Maybe, in the end, a pattern will emerge so we can predict where and when he'll strike again. But in order to get a pattern, sir, you must have quite a number of separate events. Just like drawing a graph. And, in the case of a murderer, those separate events, well, you can see what that means." The inspector was eyeing me fixedly. "Now, take Mr. Mallory. I don't suspect him. I don't think anything of the sort. But the fact remains that both these murders took place within a short distance of his house. That's the only connection, but it's also the only connection in the whole affair. So, if you'll just tell me what you know about Mallory?"

I nodded, half-chastened and half-annoyed. Peal scribbled cryptic notes as I divulged what little I knew of Mallory. I made no mention of the belly dancer in deference to John's feelings. When I had finished, Peal sighed and closed his notebook. He was understandably less than elated over the meager gleanings I had managed to impart.

"You'll be seeing Mallory tomorrow?" he asked.

"I expect so."

"I may want to speak to you again. Are you staying here at the Red Lion?"

"Registered," Mabel quickly confirmed.

I nodded.

"Thank you for your help, sir," Peal said.

After Peal had left, John and I sat for a while in silence.

"What sort of man is he, Ashley?" he asked me.

"I really don't know, John. I'm sorry."

"I don't suppose he'll hurt her?"

"Hurt her? He's not a likable man, but certainly no brute."

"Ah, I'm being foolish. I—I went out to his house once. Just after Arabella moved there. I wanted to talk with her, see if I could persuade her to come home. Ashley, she seemed, well, stupefied by the man. Dazed. As if he'd put a spell on her." He hunched his shoulders in a shrug or, perhaps, a shudder. "Well, it's not your concern. But if you go to his place—if you see her, I mean—well, if you could just make sure she's all right?"

"Of course, John."

He nodded. It was late, but he apparently had no intention of leaving the bar. Mabel had disappeared. Suddenly I felt very tired and told John I was going to bed. He made no reply. I left through the side door. Mabel was on the telephone, assuring someone that Inspector Peal himself had told her that the killer was certain to strike again.

I retired to my room.

4

That night I slept badly.

The bed was softer than I preferred and enveloped my body, while my mind played over the events of the day. I had become accustomed to the routine of my cottage. The train journey had weakened me physically and left my mind easy prey for a confusion of thoughts. I considered the paradox of a quiet village as the scene of two ghastly murders; the coincidence of meeting an old friend whose daughter had succumbed to the dubious blandishments of the same strange man I had come to see; the clatter of unseen hooves and the subsequent tale of lust and vengeance which, explaining the sounds, left them all the more inexplicable. Eventually, as I ebbed toward sleep, I even marveled at the circumstances that enabled a medieval pub to bear a modern jukebox. When at last I slept, I had a jumble of dreams on various levels through which I sank; dreams of intangible substance but cloying mood.

There was a young lad on a green bicycle. The spokes made revolving shadows in a dusty road, and this was eerie in that there was no sunlight, no other shadows, the light diffused and constant. Something moved through the trees beside the road, paralleling the youth. He pedaled faster, but whatever moved in the undergrowth kept pace. Then trees and road converged and blurred. There were rustlings and whimpers, and old Melville Coots appeared, silently mouthing a word. "Monster, monster, monster," he repeated as his face ballooned toward me, drawing so close that I lost focus, then receding to reveal that it was not Coots at all, but Arabella Cunningham, dressed in the scanty costume of a belly dancer, retreating from me with gyrating pelvis. She did not dance gracefully. She twitched like a marionette. Then she was a marionette, diminishing to a small doll jerking on strings. Lucian Mallory was working those strings. He wore Arabian robes. When he threw the cowl back, I saw that his face was swathed in brittle linen like a mummy, only his remarkable eyes exposed. I didn't dare rush after Arabella. I was afraid he would put strings on me.

Then I woke up quite abruptly and looked around the room. Dim light carried from the window and blocked the opposite wall. The painting hung askew in this rectangle of illumination, manifesting the truth of physical laws in a world of illusion. Afterward I slept again, more soundly. When I again awoke it was morning and birds were singing.

I went downstairs and encountered Mabel Sinclair passing through the reception room. She seemed cheerful. "If you'd care to go into the breakfast room, I'll be with you in just a moment," she said.

"You seem to do everything here."

"Yes, I have to. Except on Saturday nights there's a barmaid, and sometimes I have some help on Sunday lunchtime. I had a cook here last year. A Chinaman. But I had to let him go. Didn't pay. Don't get many for dinner regular, and he wasn't reasonable about adjusting his wages according to the business. Funny, that. You'd think a Chinaman would understand more about wages, being as how he was probably a coolie or something in the East. Think he'd of been thankful for the job instead of grumbling. Had quite a bit of trouble with him."

Shaking her head she started to move on.

"May I use your phone?"

"On the counter. Local call?"

"Yes. I assume so. The Croft?"

"Oh, yes. Yes, that's local. I heard you discussing Mr. Mallory with the inspector. Couldn't help overhearing. Egypt, eh?"

"Yes, that's right."

"My husband was in Egypt once."

"Is that so?"

"Oh, yes. He was a naval man, like I told you. I don't suppose you were a naval man?"

"I'm afraid not."

"Funny, you meeting Mr. Mallory in Egypt. I guess he must travel a lot. He was in the West Indies just before he came here, they say. 'Course, they say lots of things. Plenty of gossip in the village. Never met Mr. Mallory myself."

"I don't suppose he comes into the village much."

"No. No, I guess he wants his privacy. Expect that's why he took the old Hammond place. Secluded, you know. He only comes in once a fortnight or so to buy food. Got a big open motorcar, old-fashioned. Expensive, I daresay."

I smiled and attempted to move toward the desk, but she continued talking: "'Course, he spent some time here while he was making arrangements for the house. Not at the Red Lion, though. But in the village. At first it was thought he was some sort of preacher or evangelist or something. Maybe a missionary, being as how he has traveled so much. That was before the trouble at the vicar's garden party, of course—" She paused and studied me with a slight smile. She knew she'd captured my interest. I waited to hear more. She waited to be questioned. Finally she broke down and shrugged, "But who am I to pass on gossip about him? I wasn't even there, only know what I've been told."

"And what was that, Mrs. Sinclair?"

"Well, I can't rightly say—"

"All right," I said, and essayed another advance upon the telephone.

Mabel took a hurried step after me and spluttered breathlessly, "I only heard about it from a couple of the local gossips and you can't always believe them and anyhow they didn't really understand much of what went on—" I turned back. Mabel looked relieved. She continued, "The way I understand it is that your Mr. Mallory and the vicar had a terrible row. They say as Mr. Mallory had been drinking, you know. And they fell to arguing over religion. At first it was more of a discussion, but soon enough they became heated. They say Mr. Mallory deliberately provoked Grimm. He's the vicar, Grimm," she explained confidentially. "And Grimm got all excited, and what should he do but denounce Mr. Mallory as a heathen! Fancy that? Fire and brimstone talk. Didn't trouble Mr. Mallory none at all, and they say he put Grimm pretty well in his place, although I'm sure I don't know what place that would be. Got a way with him, your Mr. Mallory. All the ladies present —they were shocked at hearing him argue with the vicar, of course—but the way they described it to me, I could tell they considered Mallory quite the charmer. Anyhow, Grimm had to ask Mallory to leave in the end. All red-faced and flustered, pointing toward the gate, they say he looked like the Lord driving Adam from the Garden of Eden. Of course, that was said tongue-in-cheek, you know, not by way of sacrilege." She paused and vouchsafed a smug look, then lowered her voice conspiratorially. "And Miss Cunningham left with him—"

I stared at her.

"Just like that," she said. She tightened her lips and bobbed her head up and down, relieved of her burden of knowledge just as a weary horse is relieved of the bridle. "First time she'd ever met him, to anyone's knowledge, and she just up and left with him without a care as to what others would think."

"Yes. Well, I must make my telephone call now."

"Not that I'm speaking out against her—"

I gave her a crisp nod and walked over to the desk. Mabel went about her business. I could well imagine Mallory, drunk and aggressive, baiting some country vicar. It was quite in character. Still, his character didn't concern me, and neither, I told myself, did Arabella Cunningham's behavior. I was interested in Mallory's hieroglyphs, nothing more.

Yes, the operator informed me, Mr. Mallory had a telephone and she would ring his number. I hadn't known whether to expect him to be on the phone. Hating telephones myself, I rather presumed the same feelings in anyone immersed in the past, but then Mallory made no differentiation between past and present and certainly was the type to value convenience and expediency. The phone rang in my ear. Too bad, I thought, that my message hadn't been called through to him instead of delivered by messenger. It would have prevented the murder. But, I supposed, in this rural village the traditions of delivery were too deeply ingrained, and the telephone too recent an invention to be trusted. I wondered if a second attempt had been made to deliver the telegram. It would be quite understandable if it had been forgotten in the excitement and commotion of the circumstances, or if it proved difficult to find a second messenger to follow in the tracks of that first unfortunate lad. Then the receiver was lifted at the other end. I recognized Mallory's voice and identified myself.

"Ah, Ashley. Good of you to ring. Where are you?"

"Farriers Bar."

"What? So soon?"

"I came in on last night's train."

"But I expected you this evening. Your telegram has only just arrived—"

Curious, I asked, "Who brought it?"

"What? Why, my dear fellow, what does that matter? Some elderly lady on a bicycle."

I smiled, my faith in duty restored, imagining Emma the postmistress carrying out her task.

Mallory was saying, "You should have let me know in time. I'd have met your train."

I didn't care to detail the matter over the phone. I said, "There was a mix-up over that. No matter. I'm stopping at the Red Lion."

"Yes? Well, I've plenty of room to put you up here, Ashley. Why don't I fetch you. Noon, shall we say?"

"That will suit me."

"Good of you to come so swiftly."

"I hope it will prove worthwhile."

"Rest assured."

"Noon, then."

I proceeded into the breakfast room, a small chamber off the lobby with sunlight on yellow curtains. The tables had white cloths and plastic flowers. I was the only one there. Presently Mabel appeared for my order. She was a trifle disconcerted that I wanted coffee rather than tea and muttered as she left, something, I think, about foreign ways. She returned soon enough with an enormous breakfast which she carefully arranged before me, all good English fare. She inquired whether I'd had my telephone call, obviously curious. I nodded and asked for a newspaper. The coffee was hideous. When she returned with the paper I told her I'd changed my mind and would like some tea. She was quite happy about this. She'd brought me the local newspaper, an amateurish weekly consisting mainly of local advertisements. The front page was understandably filled with an account of the murder. It was complete but without the gory details that might have been stressed, proving there is something to be said for a village weekly which, surviving on subscription, does not rely on sensationalism.

Mabel returned with the tea, which was good; she asked if I required anything else, then went to open the bar. Several locals had already massed in the street without, patiently awaiting opening time. I glanced through the news, relieved to find no mention of who had sent the telegram—a strange guilt lingered there—and then, in a smaller article, saw that the first victim of this madman—for surely the killer was the same—had now been identified. The name was Amos Snow. He was a brain surgeon whose home and practice were in London, and it hadn't yet been determined—at least to the knowledge of the newspaper—why he had been in the Farriers Bar area. This, the article disclosed, was being investigated.

A brain surgeon, I mused.

A doctor.

Inspector Peal had asked if Mallory were a doctor, and I pondered a possible connection. It seemed tenuous at best. I finished breakfast and went out.

With the better part of two hours to wait, and not wishing to remain in my room, I strolled down the high street. It was a sunny day and pleasant, with the light on red-tiled roofs and cobblestones. I walked the length of the village and, crossing the street, came back on the other side. At the corner I found Melville Coots looking glum. He was standing outside the tobacconist's, staring at the door. The shutters were down. When I spoke, Coots blinked once and then grinned.

"Get fixed up at the Red Lion?" he asked.

"I did."

"I just came in to get my ounce of tobacco." He nodded at the door. "I reckon Brooke won't be opening today, though, seeing as he's had a tragedy."

"I suppose not."

"Can't blame him for that. I sure could fancy a smoke, though. Seems like a tobacconist has got some obligations toward his customers."

"I believe they sell tobacco at the Red Lion."

"Um. Well, I've an account here with Brooke, you know. That Mrs. Sinclair is fussy about accounts. Sort of mean, you get my meaning." He squinted at me. "Not supposed to allow credit in a pub, she says. Not that it's the money, no sir, but I wouldn't feel right giving my custom to someone else after dealing with Brooke all these years."

"I know what you mean."

"You wouldn't have any spare tobacco on you?"

"I've left my pouch in my room, I'm afraid."

Coots scowled at the locked door. I suppressed a smile. I still had time to kill, and this was an amusing old man. I said, "Actually, I was just going back to the Red Lion, so if you'd care to come along? As it happens, I was going to buy some tobacco. We might even have a pint, if you've nothing better to do?"

"Why, don't mind if I do, sir. It's a pleasure to talk with a gentleman what has a way with words."

He winked at me, his face creasing like an old leather boot that has known the stirrups and polish and, though aged, was too comfortable to be discarded. Coots squinted as the sunlight struck his upturned face, and as surely as that light, a notion fell upon me. What, when all is said and done, is the body but a well-used patch of hide? Yet we use our boots and gloves far better than we use our skins. A man may pass his boots on to his son, but his body is consigned to the tomb. In our Christian world there is no respect for the leather envelope which seals our souls; we cast it into the earth to nourish worms, or into the furnace to feed the flames.

My own flesh crawled with premonition, my living fibers rebelled against predestined corruption. I grimaced. It would be far more proper to be devoured by filed-toothed cannibals; better the voracious shark than the sluggish worm, better still to be preserved for the aeons by the ancient Egyptian rites than to gratify the necrophagous scavengers of the grave. Coots said something. I saw his lips move but heard no sound. Another sound had filled my ears from within, the sodden soft sound of decay. Was this akin to the dead cries I had twice heard vibrating from barren stone? What turned my mind to timeless mummies in eternal crypts? Was it some adumbration of Mallory's meaning that had registered unknown in my memory? Whatever, it was an eerie chill on a sunlit street, and I shook my head to drive away the fantasy. A body, after all, could not be passed on like a pair of gloves.

Coots spoke again.

This time I heard him clearly.

"Are you all right, sir?"

I nodded and smiled.

"Shall we be getting along, then?"

We walked off, Coots bouncing along beside me. There was little enough flesh on his aged bones. We crossed the street and turned into the Red Lion.

We took stools at the bar, and Mabel drew two pints. A youth in a leather jacket was playing the jukebox, but the decibel level was mercifully subdued. The two dart players from the night before, joined by another pair, were at it again, and several other customers lounged at tables. Sunlight streamed through the frosted windows, and the room presented a cheerful, sociable appearance. Thinking about the strange premonition that had come over me in the street, I felt rather silly. Coots sipped his beer and, with froth on his upper lip, drew out his blackened briar and placed it on the bar. The only tobacco for sale was a wretched navy cut, but I bought an ounce and offered it to my companion. He carefully broke the dry flat sheets and stuffed his pipe to the brim. I gave him a box of matches, and he struck one. It flared. Mabel leaned on the bar and drawled, "Do you reckon it's true, what the inspector was saying last night?"

"What would that be?"

"About the madman attacking again?"

"It's possible."

Coots, still holding the flame to his pipe, raised his eyebrows. Smoke trailed past his jaw.

"Eh? Peal said that, did he?"

"He did. Right here at this bar he did," Mabel added.

Coots turned to me with his brow still up.

"He said that, did he?"

Mabel glared at him.

"What I just told you."

"Well," I interposed, "he said it was possible."

"Seems to me that would imply the work of a monster, right enough."

"Ah, come off that monster stuff," Mabel told him. "Just 'cause you've had a bit of glory finding a dead man—"

"Not just any dead man. A proper victim."

"Why do you suppose the inspector was asking all them questions about Mr. Mallory?" Mabel asked me.

"Oh, as he said. He's inquiring about all the new residents. And, of course, both murders took place near The Croft, so I suppose he wondered if Mallory might not have heard or seen something. Nothing more than that, surely."

Coots had his pipe burning well now, and the plumes of smoke spiraled upward. "The Croft, eh?" he retorted. "There's plenty of woodland around there, that's why. Monsters need a place to go to earth."

"Will you give off that monster talk?" Mabel said sharply, and I suddenly realized she was not annoyed at something she considered nonsense; rather that she was, if not frightened, at least unnerved. Coots regarded her mildly. It was difficult to assess how serious he was. His eyes were bright, but his face inscrutable as he said, "Mind you, there's something strange about that house, I'll give you that. Always been an eerie old place. And since the new tenant moved in—" He turned toward me with the same bland expression while Mabel listened with her mouth agape. "I've had occasion, while on the course of my private affairs, to pass close by that house several times in the dead of night." He winked. Whether this signal concerned the truth of his tale or the nature of his private affairs, I couldn't say. "Always had lights burning there, no matter what the hour."

Mabel was dissatisfied with this, for it was feeble gossip.

"What's wrong with that?" she demanded. "Nothing strange about lights. It's the dark you got to fear."

"That's as may be. There are those to whom the dark is a

friend and a succor. But somehow it always gave me an odd feeling, seeing those windows lighted up in the middle of the night. It's a big old house, you see, set back from the road, with trees around it. Looks strange enough in the daylight. But in the dark, with the whole building in shadows and those squares of bright light—well, it gives a man to wonder what they might be doing there."

Mabel assumed a censorious expression.

"Ah, you're always snooping around, Coots. Lighted windows, indeed. What's that to do with you, eh? Sneak up and have a look in, did you?"

"I never! Me? I never looked in no windows, Mabel. I never even looked in your kitchen windows—"

Mabel appeared suspicious. Coots appeared innocent. "Still and all," she continued finally, "it wouldn't surprise me to hear they were carrying on to all hours out at that place. After the way he stole that nice Cunningham girl off with never a thought for her poor father or her reputation. It's getting as bad as cities here, these days. Free love and what they call orgies and suchlike."

"What would you know about orgies?" Coots asked.

"Well, I'm sure I never sneaked around looking in no windows to find out," Mabel sniffed. She turned to me. "I meant nothing disrespectful about that Cunningham girl, you know. Whatever people like is fine with me. Other people, I mean. People are just different, that's all."

"That's true enough," Coots agreed. "You take this monster, now. He's just got to be different from you or me. Simply has to be. You can't tell me no different. 'Course, if he's a proper monster, with fangs and bristling hair and yellow eyes, then it's obvious." He paused to stare at Mabel. She moved slightly away. "But just suppose he's only a monster on the insides? How about that, eh? Suppose he looks just like anyone else on the outside, but he's got a monster's heart? What about a monster's guts? Eh? Why, he'd fool you every time.

You might even have served him a drink, for all you know. Lots of drinks. How would that make you feel, knowing your beer was being poured down into monster guts?"

"Leave off!" Mabel squeaked.

Coots shrugged. He turned toward me.

"I got to thinking about it after our converse last night, sir. I was keen on the monster theory, as you know, but then I got to wondering if it mightn't be a foreigner?"

"How you figure that?" Mabel asked.

"Why, it's plain as the nose on your face," Coots told her. "Even if it is a monster, it could still be a foreigner. Pretty well have to be, come to that. The English don't run much to monsters. But alien lands, disgorging their immigrants onto us—who knows? The Balkans and Africa and the like. What do we know about the way they are inside?"

"We do have a few foreigners around these days," Mabel replied, obviously more comfortable with immigrants than monsters. "Some gypsies, too."

"There you go."

Coots puffed wisely at his pipe stem.

"I wonder if I should express this opinion to Inspector Peal?" he mused.

"I'm sure he's considered it," I said.

"Of course, it might be thought of as prejudice. Wouldn't want to give that impression. More like postjudice, I reckon. But the more I think about it—yes, sir, I'll just bet that's what it is. Most likely one of them blackamoors, being as how they come from Africa. Lots of wild and savage beasts in Africa, you know. And monsters have got a lot of the wild beast in them. Have to have, acting the way they do."

Mabel began to apprehend that she was having her leg pulled.

"Ah, black men are the same as white men," she said.

Coots squinted.

"How you know that?" he asked.

"They just is, is all."

"You never had nothing to do with no blackamoors, did you?"

She looked indignant.

" 'Course not. I just heard tell."

"What about Chinamen, then?"

"Chinamen!" she squawked.

Coots went to the toilet.

"Who does he think he is, coming that Chinamen stuff with me? Chinamen, indeed."

I ordered two more pints. Coots returned. Mabel took a stand at the other end of the bar. I looked at my wristwatch. It was exactly noon, and through the door, gaunt in a long black robe, appeared Lucian Mallory. He smiled and conferred upon me a nod that he suffered to resemble a bow. He didn't approach the bar but stood beside the door. I excused myself and walked over toward him. He was still smiling. Behind me I heard Mabel say, "See here, Coots, you old bugger, what's all this about Chinamen then?" We proceeded out, and I didn't hear his reply. I had left the tobacco on the bar.

"Well, Ashley," said Lucian Mallory, as we stepped into the street. "It's been a while, eh? What? Four, five years now?" He touched my arm lightly in a somewhat embarrassing gesture of familiarity. He was a towering figure, and I was obliged to peer upward into his cuneate face. The sun was very nearly overhead, and our shadows had become irregular pools flowing from our boots. His eye sockets were masked ovals.

"Four, I think."

"Yes. Yes, four long years."

"Long years, Mallory? I rather thought you considered time static?"

He looked surprised, then laughed.

"You astound me, Ashley. So you've remembered my theories, eh? I must have impressed you more than it seemed. No, that's not right, rather you are a more intelligent fellow than I thought you in Egypt. But I know that now, of course. Had I realized your learning, I'd have been less—condescending? —in our discourse."

I stared at him, flushing faintly. This was the man who had seduced John's young daughter, who had the audacity to speak of condescension concerning his metaphysical and amateur concepts. I thought that I had been rather tolerant with him, actually, and started to reply sharply. Then I realized he had meant no insult. It was merely his manner. He was trying to be friendly; in his strange way he was asking forgiveness for underestimating me. A curious man, indeed. Keeping my voice level, I replied, "I'd not noticed your condescension, and if such were intended I'm afraid it passed over me."

He laughed again, a staccato bark.

"Ah well, it's true that time is static. My theories haven't changed. But we are not static, you know. We are forced by physical laws to move through constant time, and for us that motion can be long. Let us say, then, that four years is a long journey."

"Agreed."

"It was good of you to come."

"Do I understand you've been in the West Indies all this while?"

"Two years. Haiti. A remarkable country."

"Is that culture another of your interests?"

Mallory appeared puzzled, then smiled slightly. "It's all the same interest," he said. "My findings in Egypt sent me to Haiti. All things are connected, you know, and to understand one thing fully is to be led to another."

"I should have thought the scope of modern knowledge precludes the Renaissance man?"

"Ah, quite the contrary. It's all a muddle now, I admit, but when each branch of knowledge is extended to the limits I think you will find that they meet; that one master law will govern everything."

"Quite possible. But surely that's for the mathematicians to run through the labyrinth?"

"Ah, the hounds of cryptic numbers," he replied. "Advancing the magic squares of the ancients. Mathematicians are fools, they'd rather divide than multiply and abstract rather than clarify and what do they know of common denominators? Ah well. Shall we go?"

I nodded. His Bentley was parked at the curb, and he guided me toward it with a hand on my shoulder. There was no chauffeur. I was rather surprised that Mallory should drive his own vehicle and asked, "Is Sam Cooper still with you?"

"Well, yes, he is," he said distractedly. He opened the door for me, then closed it and crossed in front of the hood to slide in behind the wheel. It was a fine car, old and well cared for. As he put the keys in the ignition, I commented, "I rather liked Sam. Of course, I only met him the once—"

"I'm afraid you'll find Sam changed."

"Oh?"

"He met with an accident."

I looked at him, waiting. My host was fingering the keys but hadn't turned them; he seemed to be meditating, and then said, "There was some brain damage. Rather serious."

I felt a chill, a solid clunk of circumstances. Amos Snow, brain surgeon. "Of course," I said, "you've had him looked at by doctors?"

"Of course. It's hopeless, however. He's become quite incapable of caring for himself."

"I see. Well, it's good of you to keep him on under such circumstances," I replied, considering it not in character for Mallory to concern himself over a servant's misfortune. He shrugged and turned the key. The motor started smoothly. Thinking of Arabella, I added, "I suppose you have to have a nurse for him?"

"Not really," he said, and then as if to change the subject, muttered apologetically, "But this was unfortunate about your telegram, Ashley. A mix-up, you said?"

"You've not heard about the murder?"

He began to engage the lever solidly into gear.

"What? Oh, this Amos Snow affair. Yes, but—"

"No, the second murder."

He stiffened. He had already pressed the accelerator, and now his foot pushed on the clutch so that the motor whined in neutral and the car remained stationary. His head swiveled around toward me like an automaton. "What did you say? What murder?"

"I'm afraid so. The same madman, apparently. He killed the lad who was delivering my telegram. Yesterday, sometime."

"I see."

He looked away and sat silently for a moment, affected far more profoundly than I'd have thought.

"Yes, it was rather gruesome," I said, to break the silence. He nodded absently. Then, abruptly he blurted, "But see here, Ashley. I've made rather a mistake. I shan't be able to put you up tonight."

It required a moment for this to sink in. I stared dumbly at his profile. His lips were drawn back, and his teeth showed in ivory blocks.

"Silly of me, eh?" he said. "I suppose I was excited at the prospect of having the translations made. Truth is, there's no room at the house. I'm terribly sorry."

I was dumbfounded, then I was angry. My face had become suffused with a crimson commingling of embarrassment and indignation.

"Oh? I'd understood it was a large house?"

"Well, yes, you know, but I've closed off all the extra rooms. With only Sam and me—"

"And Miss Cunningham," I added coldly.

Mallory frowned. His lips closed slowly.

"You're well informed," he said.

"It's a small village."

"Am I such an interesting topic in this wretched place, then?"

"I know her father."

"I see. Yes. I'm afraid he doesn't approve. Well, that's nothing to me." He turned toward me again. "There's nothing between us, Ashley. Nothing that these local buffoons would imagine. Arabella helps me care for Sam."

"If that is true, Mallory, it would greatly ease her father's mind if he were so told."

"What do I care for her father's mind?" he snapped. "As I said, it's nothing to me. Let him think as he will, I have more important concerns than soothing the outraged morality of some fool—"

"Mallory, he is my friend."

"Ah, quite. Forgive me. Tell him, if you like. It's the absolute truth, for that matter."

I nodded. I almost believed him, although a sudden taunting image of his belly dancer pirouetted provocatively through my thoughts. "Well, if it's not convenient, then," I sighed, and placed my hand on the door handle.

"Wait. I've been offensive. I can put you up, certainly, but I'll have to open another room. Suppose I arrange it and pick you up tomorrow?"

"As you like. I don't mind opening a room for myself."

"Oh, that would never do," he said, in his curious way of being civil. "Only the delay—can you translate from a photographic copy?"

I shrugged.

"If it's a good one. The content, you understand. Not the period or the age. The stylus marks wouldn't mean much in a two-dimensional copy."

"Yes, yes. The content." He deliberated for a moment, biting his lip. "Let me suggest, then, that I run out to the house and fetch a copy of one of the tablets. You can begin working on it here at the Red Lion while I'm arranging your accommodations. Will that suit you?"

I turned up a palm. Tempted to refuse and to depart on the next train, I nevertheless was more greatly tempted by the prospect of examining Mallory's findings—perhaps, to my discredit, I was tempted most of all by the possibility of determining that his discoveries were of little value and the satisfaction it should give me duly to inform him. I could imagine, pleasurably, his reaction.

"That will be satisfactory," I said.

"I'll return in an hour, then."

I nodded and opened the door. The engine was still turning over smoothly like a stalking beast faintly trembling as its prey crouched at the curb. As I got out Mallory leaned across the front seat.

"I hope you'll not think too badly of me for my thoughtlessness," he said. He seemed genuinely concerned. "I have a great deal on my mind. Things far more important than graciousness. I'm sure you'll understand, Ashley."

"Of course," I said.

He nodded, and I closed the door. He drove off immediately and hurriedly, without looking back. I watched the big car lurch as it careened around the corner. A strange, strange man. I walked back to the Red Lion.

John Cunningham had come into the bar while I had been with Mallory. Red-eyed and pale, he was seated at a table by the frosted window. There was a glass of brandy in front of him, and he brooded with his hands flat on the table, one on either side of his drink. Bars of sunlight passed over his forearms and, striking the brandy glass, refracted as though from a prism. He had shaved, but not well, as if he'd made the effort but had given up halfway through. I wondered how late into the night he'd continued drinking, keeping Mrs. Sinclair in the bar or perhaps taking a bottle to his room. When I went over to his table he peered up from the tops of his eyes. He nodded, and I sat directly across the small circular table.

"Thought you'd gone out to Mallory's?" he said.

"Evidently he wasn't prepared for a houseguest."

"That so?"

"John—" I sought words, "I mentioned Arabella. Mallory assures me there's nothing between them; that she's merely working for him."

A glimmer appeared in his red-veined eyes, a brief sharp flicker like flint struck on hope. Then he grunted.

"You'd believe that swine?"

"I've no reason not to."

"Arabella told me the same thing," he muttered thought-fully. He raised his glass and turned it about, transforming the light patterns on the table. The sunlight fanned and faded, then again coalesced into a bar, bright and solid. "When I went out to The Croft, she seemed almost surprised that I'd suppose they were—what?—lovers?"

"Well, then? You may well doubt Mallory's word, but why disbelieve Arabella?"

"Because she didn't seem much interested in making her point. She just brushed it aside, treated my concern en passant, as it were. Surely, if she really was merely working for him, she'd have taken the trouble to convince me?"

His misgivings were eminently understandable, of course, but I demurred, "She's a woman now, John. Perhaps she feels you no longer have influence on her morality. Perhaps, even, her present condition seemed so patently obvious that it never occurred to her you'd doubt her statement."

He considered this.

"Yes, I can see that with Arabella. But why, Ashley? If it's just a question of employment? Why in heaven's name would she take a job with Mallory? She certainly didn't lack for money. She wouldn't have left home for that reason. What on earth could she do? She's no maid, Ashley, no housekeeper, what possible duties could she have?"

"People grow up, John. Maybe she just felt it was time to strike out on her own?"

"Maybe," he said doubtfully. "It was my fault. I can understand that. She grew up faster than I realized. I still considered her a child, and she was a woman. She must have been miserable, living with me. Perhaps she saw herself growing into a spinster, eh? Spending her life caring for a helpless, aging father? Then that scoundrel, with his glib tongue—" He grimaced. "Should that make me feel better, Ashley? To imagine that she wasn't going to him but going away from me?"

"I don't know."

"Um. She may well have been concerned about growing old, you know. Sometimes the young are. Her mother died so young. And she had no companions her own age at the house."

"But Mallory is as old as you, John."

"Not her father, however. And with his talk of immortality and eternal youth—"

"What?"

He regarded me with mild surprise.

"Don't tell me the good Mrs. Sinclair hasn't filled you in on the gossip?"

"She mentioned some difficulty at the vicar's."

"Yes. She would. I wasn't there, of course, but I asked Grimm about it afterward. Mallory had some half-baked ideas about living forever, or not growing old, something like that. Wild enough to give Grimm apoplexy. Not that I think Mallory was serious, you know; probably just having a jest at the vicar's expense, or else, as he did, trying to impress the ladies. Heresy, Grimm called it." John smiled sadly. "Why eternal life should be heresy when an afterlife is divine eludes me. But then, I'm no theologian."

He downed his brandy.

I went to the bar and asked for a pint. Coots was still seated there and proffered me a grizzled grin. The tobacco package was no longer on the bar. The youth had abandoned the juke-box to bubbling silence. I asked Mabel to give Coots another beer, and John called, "Get me a brandy, would you, Ashley?" As I glanced at him, he was staring down at his hands, and I couldn't refuse the request. Mabel sighed and registered an unspoken reproach, then shrugged and poured the brandy. I carried the drinks back to our table, from which vantage point I could monitor the street. We sat without speaking for a while, and John drank with short, steady sips while his eyes grew ever narrower, too narrow for his broad face. I told him I'd be going out to The Croft on the morrow and that I'd find a chance to talk with Arabella.

"Mallory might well have been truthful," I added.

John nodded. Whatever hope he fostered was forlorn to his mind. After a time he rose and went to the bar. He walked steadily, so steadily that I could tell he was expending great effort. Mabel refilled his glass without protest. There was no objection she could make, nor I. How does one offer unwanted advice to a friend? How does one know what dark dragons have slunk slavering into another man's mind? I never had a daughter.

I heard an automobile turn at the corner and, thinking it inadvisable for John to encounter Mallory, excused myself and retired from the bar. John seemed unaware of my departure. I went out to the street. Mallory was driving, and someone sat beside him. I raised a hand, but Mallory was peering intently ahead with his predator's vision and failed to notice me on the sidewalk. He didn't stop at the curb this time, but turned in under the archway. I observed that his companion was Sam Cooper. Like Mallory, Sam was looking straight ahead, sitting very stiff and still. He too failed to see me. I walked down the arch after the car. This time the old stones echoed only the exhaust.

Mallory swung the vehicle around in the courtyard and quickly got out. He advanced to meet me with a large manila envelope in his hand.

"Here we are," he said. "I brought only one copy. Not the most vital, but it should enable you to determine if you can make these translations."

I accepted the envelope. Mallory waited for me to open it. I nodded at the car.

"Isn't that Sam?"

"Yes."

"May I speak to him?"

"There's little point. He won't recognize you."

"I'd like to see."

Mallory gave an exasperated shrug, and I walked over to the side of the car. Sam didn't turn. He stared out the windshield. He was heavily bundled and wore gloves, although the day was warm.

"Sam? Remember me?"

No response.

"Thomas Ashley. We met in Egypt."

He completely ignored me.

I leaned down to intercept his vision. His countenance afforded me a shock. He seemed blind; his eyes were wide open but appeared to have no focal point. His mouth hung agape, and a thin trickle of spittle ran down from each corner, dissecting his jaw from lips to chin. He looked like a hinged puppet awaiting the ventriloquist's voice.

I winced, recalling the lively fellow chatting under the desert cliff, his quote from Churchill, his respect for Mallory. I took out my handkerchief and wiped his chin. Nothing happened. Mallory's shadow curved up the side of the car as he approached behind me.

"As I told you, it's quite hopeless."

"This is terrible."

"Yes, terrible."

"What sort of accident was it?"

"He struck his head."

I stared at Mallory. "That's all? It must have been a tremendous blow."

"Yes. He tripped and fell down a flight of stairs."

"Where did this happen? When?"

"Here. At The Croft. Oh, I forget, some months ago. What does it matter, it's done."

"I'm concerned, naturally."

"There's nothing to be done."

"It's permanent?"

"Oh, yes. Quite."

There seemed some hidden meaning in the simple words.

"You said he'd been examined by doctors?"

"Of course."

"An expert?" I asked, and although I hadn't intended it, the question may have sounded loaded. Mallory regarded me for what seemed an extended interval, then his eyes flicked away in their shadowed sockets. "Yes," he said, "one of the best. In point of fact, although it's none of your concern, it was this brain surgeon from London."

This information didn't immediately register.

"Snow," he added. "The murder victim."

"What! Is that what he was doing down here?"

"Yes."

"You've informed the authorities, of course?"

He smiled.

"Ah, the authorities, those sterling fellows who confuse descriptive law with statute and mistake eternal truths for traffic violations. The authorities, of course, had already ascertained why Snow was here. I verified it, yes. It seems it was just after he'd left my house that he met with this madman. I almost said, 'with his fate.' Strange how the platitudes persist, eh? But it was a sorry thing. He was a competent man." He paused, then seemed to feel the need to add, "If only he'd allowed me to drive him to the station, he would have lived. But it was a fine day, and he decided to walk. Still, I suppose, with a madman—if it hadn't been Snow, it would have been someone else."

I glanced back at Sam. His face was still distorted, and a renewed supply of saliva had begun sliding down from the corners of his mouth. His nostrils were flared and seemed unaffected by his breathing, which was so quiet as to be imperceptible.

"Aren't you going to look at the photocopy?"

I nodded and opened the envelope. The text was large and clear. I ran my eyes over the runic symbols, and Mallory watched with great interest.

"Yes, I can manage this."

He took a deep breath, relieved.

"This isn't a copy of the most valuable writings, you understand," he iterated.

"I wondered why you trusted me with a copy," I retorted, not without sarcasm.

"I'd attempted a translation myself, but the symbols seem to vary from—"

I gestured, implying the point was insignificant.

"Well then, until tomorrow?"

"Yes."

"You might ring me when you've finished."

"I'll do that."

He hesitated.

"And, Ashley—you'll keep the translation confidential, won't you?"

"Confidential? Surely something like this? The object is valuable, granted, but a photographic copy—what need is there for secrecy?"

"Please believe me."

"Well, I have no reason not to keep it confidential," I told him. "Or did you suppose I would tell Mrs. Sinclair all about it?

Let her reveal the mysteries of ancient Egypt to the village?"

He smiled. I wondered if he wished to reserve the glory of his findings for himself, or if perhaps the papyruses and tablets had been illegally exported from Egypt; even if, however unlikely, they might have been stolen from some museum. But these speculations were of little concern to me.

"Yes, I'll ring you," I said.

He walked around and entered the car. When he started the engine, Sam jerked as if the vibrations had reverberated up his backbone; as if he were a component of the machine, susceptible to external impulse but a void within his mind. I shook my head, deeply regretting his hopeless condition. Mallory put the car in gear, and I stepped back. He let in the clutch, and the Bentley rolled toward the arch. At that very moment, John Cunningham stepped out from the side door of the Red Lion.

5

With preternatural acuity, I saw those snorting black horses, the betrayed husband's wild eyes and bared teeth as he lashed them on under the arch, then heard the startled cry of his wife and her lover as they succumbed to the churning coach. I cried out. In that instant I was absolutely certain that the past was to be reenacted; that John would die under those tires as had the illicit lovers under the wheels. Then Mallory slammed on the brakes. The car halted, shuddering, squatting low on the back springs. The radiator stopped scant inches from my friend.

John looked up, startled, then belatedly leaped back with the drunkard's delayed reaction. I exhaled with relief. John shook his head and blinked vacuously; he started to wave the automobile past but then leaned closer, peering through the windshield. He hadn't understood who was in the car or where I had gone. He had simply been staggering back to his room, already befuddled by brandy. Now he recognized Mallory. His lips drew back and his eyes blazed as if the alcohol he'd consumed had suddenly ignited within his skull, burning behind his eyes with a furious glow.

He advanced on the car, blocking the exit.

I rushed up to intercept him.

Mallory leaned out the window.

"Stand aside," he commanded.

John placed one hand on the hood of the Bentley and leaned down toward Mallory.

"You," he said.

"You are in my path, sir," sneered Mallory.

"And I'll damned well stay in your path," John seethed. He suddenly had become the man I'd known before, quite capable if necessary of violent action. "Is it true, Mallory? What you told Ashley?"

He hadn't noticed me.

I started to grasp his arm, then halted, my hand extended. I couldn't blame him; why should I stop him? Mallory stared at him with a strange expression, not quite pity, but not precisely disdain. Then Mallory spoke softly. "As it happens, it is true," he said. "Now, my man, will you stand aside?"

John frowned and remained where he was.

"You are disgustingly drunk," Mallory said.

John blinked as if he couldn't believe this. Then, moving with alacrity, he grasped Mallory by the collar and threw open the door. Mallory squawked. His sudden affright pleased me, and I stepped back, unwilling to play his savior. A powerful man, John Cunningham wrenched him from the car and turned him in one motion against the wall. He held him there. Mallory was tall and his body bent, describing the curve of the stone arch at his back. His long black coattails flapped like a raven's wings, and his fingers writhed in wild gesticulation. John held him with one hand and doubled the other into a fist.

"Now you'll answer me with a civil tongue, you bastard," he cried.

Mallory's mouth worked, but he was not replying to John. He uttered an incoherent cry, obviously terrified far more than the circumstances justified.

I smiled.

Then Sam moved.

He had been so still, a mindless mass of inorganic matter, and now he was instantly transformed into a thing of blinding motion. He groped across the front seat and up from the door, rising behind John on taut thighs. His countenance was still idiotic, but now some terrible light had animated his eyes.

I shouted a warning.

John half turned, and Sam struck him across the jaw. It was an openhanded blow, hardly more than a slap in the dynamics of such motion, and yet John was hurled from his feet. He flew through the air, his hand still clenched at Mallory's collar so that a banner of black cloth was torn away, fluttering behind him.

I moved to catch him before he struck the ground, and he rammed into me with great force. I am as strong as the next man, but I could not halt that impetus. I fell backward with John sprawled crosswise over my knees. The cobblestones grated against my back. I was stunned. I placed my hands beneath me and levered myself into a sitting position with John still lying across my lap.

I looked up into the most fearsome sight I have ever beheld—

Sam was crouched over us.

His face was now beyond the idiotic, beyond even the bestial. It was superhuman. His mouth was still open but no longer slack. It was drawn into a hideous grimace. His nostrils flared wide, black. His eyes were suffused with some dark unnatural lust. As I gazed into this terrible face, my flesh froze, I could not move. John groaned weakly. Sam grasped for my throat—

His hands came out, fingers drawn into talons, and fastened on my neck. They closed with tremendous power, wrenching me from my stupor. I started to resist, but his strength was incredible. He drew me up from the ground. John tumbled from my legs. Sam hauled me upward as though I were weightless; lifted me up toward that fiendish face, those bared fangs—I cried out, but the sound came smothered as his fingers dug into my throat. My mind spun in terror. My vision blurred, background fading, so that only an inhuman face was in focus, lowering closer, closer, turning slightly to commit his mouth to my throat.

Then I was on the stones, trembling.

Mallory was standing over me, one hand on Sam's chest, holding him back and shouting wordlessly, a command more primitive than the verbal. Over his shoulder I could see Sam's face. His countenance dissolved slowly, by degrees, eyes dimming and mouth growing slack, until once again he had assumed the aspect of an imbecile.

When Mallory pointed to the car, Sam turned docilely and staggered in.

"Good God," I sobbed.

Mallory assisted me to my feet.

John was on his hands and knees, head lowered, his hair hanging down to the cobblestones over his declined brow. He was moaning.

"Are you all right?" Mallory asked.

"I—think so. I—what in the name of God caused him to act that way?"

"He doesn't act. He reacts."

"But—it was—" I was brushing my clothes, still a bit stunned, as if it were important to remove the dust.

"Sam is very loyal to me," Mallory said.

"But he was inhuman."

"He is an imbecile."

"More than that—"

"Why seek the supernatural in a deranged mind?" Mallory replied, reasonably enough. "We all have that inherent fear of the deranged, of course. But that's all it is. It was unfortunate that your—friend—sought to attack me."

Sam was motionless in the car. I turned and helped John to rise. His jaw hung open in ironic echo of Sam's, and his eyes were dazed.

"You'd better have a doctor look at him," Mallory said. "I'll accept the responsibility. Although it wasn't my fault, of course. He did attack me. Sam was just the faithful dog, protecting his master."

"We aren't troubled about responsibility," I told him. Now that my shock had ebbed, I was angry. "I'll see to John. You'd better take Sam away. Whatever possessed you to bring him into town?"

"He would have been peaceful enough. I didn't wish to leave him unattended."

"Unattended?" I said, then started. "My God. Arabella lives in the same house as he? She's alone with him at times? Mallory, how can—"

"Oh, she is quite safe. Sam has become rather devoted to her, actually."

"But my God, man, you just saw—I can't allow her to take a chance like that—"

"You can't prevent it, you mean," he observed with an amused sneer that faded abruptly. He stooped, picked up the manila envelope from where it had fallen, and handed it to me. His tone had moderated as he said, "But, you are quite right, of course. I hadn't realized how potentially dangerous Sam has become. He had never acted that way before, as you may well imagine. I'll take all precautions in the future, I assure you."

"That is advisable."

"I deeply regret this incident—and your friend's behavior, which caused it."

That enraged me. John was tottering dazedly at my side, still stunned. I retorted, "And which caused you a moment of intense discomfort, eh? You were certainly frightened, Mallory, before you were rescued."

Mallory appeared surprised.

"Did you think I was afraid of him? That I feared physical violence? You judge me harshly, my friend. I fear only death. But death can come by accident, by misadventure, when one deals with violent men. And I choose to avoid the near occasions of death until—until my work is finished."

I shrugged and turned to examine John.

"Well, then. Until tomorrow?"

I nodded.

"I'll come to get you when you're ready. You needn't worry about Sam."

I ignored him. Mallory strode across the courtyard and reentered his car. The Bentley hurtled out from the arch, neither passenger looking back. John was recovering his senses, shaking his head. I put my arm around his shoulders and helped him back into the bar.

Mabel looked up and gasped.

Coots turned, his pipe smoldering, smiling until he saw us. Then his face jolted with shock. I assisted John to a table and said, "You'd better phone for the doctor, Mabel." She nodded and hastened out, one hand at her throat. Coots came over slowly, holding his pipe in hand. He seemed concerned and, withal, strangely frightened.

"What's happened?" he asked.

"There's been an accident," I said. How readily that word comes to mind, how conveniently it resists explanation. Sam had had an accident too, Mallory had said. It is a word which covers a multitude of meaning. Coots was peering intently into John's face, bending over him.

"No need to worry," I said.

"It's not that," Coots muttered. "It's the look of his jaw."

"Yes, it seems rather a nasty injury."

"Didn't mean that," said Coots.

I looked at him. He was still gaping at John. He spoke through his teeth, as if the pipe yet were clenched there. "The corpse I found in the woods," he said. "That's just the way the jaw looked on the corpse."

Dr. Plum was a fragile birdlike man with a watch chain across his waistcoat and an air of perpetual efficiency. I waited outside John's room while he conducted his examination. My neck had begun to ache where Sam's gauntleted fingers had penetrated, but there seemed to be no serious damage beyond the bruising. Presently Plum emerged, a dapper man whose shoes gleamed like reflectors.

"Is he all right?" I asked.

"He's sleeping now. I administered a sedative."

"His jaw—"

"Was broken, yes. I've wired it up. Unpleasant, but a clean break, there should be no difficulties other than the normal discomfort." Plum peered up at me. "It must have been a powerful blow?"

"Strangely, it didn't look hard. Casually, almost."

"Um. Must've been mighty."

I agreed.

"Now, shall we see about you?"

"I'm all right."

"Your throat there. Those marks."

"Just bruises."

"Um. This is all most peculiar."

We headed for the stairs.

"Could he have been an exponent of one of those foreign styles of combat?"

"I shouldn't think so. Don't know where he'd have learned it. Very English. He was in the army—"

"Oh, yes? Well, perhaps that would account for it then. Commando training or some such, eh? Too bad they can't deactivate these types before they turn them loose on society."

We descended the staircase.

Constable Chive was talking with Mabel at the reception desk. I assumed she had summoned him on her own initiative. He had taken off his helmet and was mopping his brow. He approached us at the foot of the stairs, gazing meaningfully at Plum.

"He'll be all right," said the doctor.

Chive turned to me.

"Will you be making any charges, sir?"

"No."

"And Mr. Cunningham?"

"No, I think not."

"All right to speak to him now, Dr. Plum?"

"He's sleeping."

"I see. Well, now. What caused this attack, sir?"

I hesitated, wondering what misinformation Mabel had passed on, then uttered feebly, "A misunderstanding."

Chive waited for further explanation.

"Obviously the man is not responsible for his actions," I said. "It might be advisable if he were put away somewhere where he couldn't endanger anyone else. But that is hardly your concern."

"No, sir, it is not."

"It was a private matter."

Chive nodded and once again donned his helmet. He must have known about Mallory and Arabella, but his face remained expressionless. I was thinking about Mallory. I had given him credit for exhibiting humanitarian concern over an unfortunate servant when it would have been far less bother to have him committed; now I saw the relationship in a different perspective. Sam might be an imbecile, but he could have his uses. I recalled how terrified Mallory had appeared when threatened by John Cunningham. I'd not thought him the cowardly type, but the fact was evident in his face, and with his abrasive personality, he might well find it expedient to retain Sam as a sort of bodyguard. I nonetheless doubted whether one could bring charges against Sam, for it was indisputable that John had initiated the assault. It was fortunate that Mallory had been able to restrain him.

I touched my neck.

Very fortunate.

I followed Plum and the constable out into the street. The latter walked off behind his shadow, while Plum blinked once and glanced in the opposite direction. "I'll walk along with you, Doctor," I said. "I could use some air."

"Quite right. Air and exercise, that's what men need. I'm not so sure about excitement, though." He smiled. We strolled casually side by side. "Funny thing. I've been in practice here the better part of forty years, never had much excitement, everybody dies in bed. Now we've suddenly had two murders and this assault. Not that this is comparable to the murders, of course, but still it's exciting." We were moving into the afternoon angles, the toes of his shoes casting light like twin mirrors. "Curious how things come in cycles."

"Like epidemics."

"Just so. The epidemics of contingency."

Casually, I asked, "Were you called when Sam Cooper had his accident?"

"How's that?"

"When he suffered the brain damage?"

"Why, no. I knew nothing of that. His—condition—was caused physically, then?"

"So Mallory told me."

"Recently?"

"I believe so."

"I meant—since they've been here?"

"Oh, yes."

"Now isn't that curious?"

"How's that, Doctor?"

"Why, I've never been called out to The Croft. An accident serious enough—"

"Is there not another doctor in Farriers Bar?"

"No. Nor nearby, come to that."

I pursed my lips. Why, I wondered, had the doctor not been summoned immediately when Sam sustained his fall? With such extensive damage he must have been close to death, and why would Mallory wait until he could get Snow all the way from London? Then I shrugged. He obviously wasn't fond of the village residents, and that may have included the doctor. He had an automobile and most likely had driven Sam to the nearest hospital. That had to be the explanation, for surely he wouldn't have failed to obtain an immediate diagnosis.

Plum interrupted my thoughts.

"I wonder how it is that the man has so much strength if his brain was physically injured? To strike such a powerful blow implies he has not only strength, but reflexes as well. But those conditions are hardly in accord with brain damage which has been externally inflicted. The one seems to preclude the other." He deliberated the matter, taking small steps. "Insanity, yes, that would not affect his physical prowess —in many cases it enhances it, actually. You've heard of the incredible strength which madmen often possess. By madmen I mean those unfortunates who by reason of chemical imbalance within their own brain become deranged. However, if Sam Cooper suffered physical damage to his brain tissue— why, that invariably results in loss of facilities—they become uncoordinated, lose the power of speech, blurred vision, things like that. I can't see how an accident could actually increase a man's physical prowess. Still, there are many things which I don't know and can't see. That doesn't mean they aren't there, eh?" He gave a deprecating smile. We walked on, passing the tobacconist at the corner. It was still closed, the metal grate lowered before the door. Plum seemed to be thinking further.

"I suppose this altercation concerned Cunningham's daughter, did it not?"

I nodded.

"Yes. Thought as much. Not very difficult to figure that out, was it? Same as his drinking. Cunningham's, I mean. Suppose I shouldn't mention that, really, but I'm sure you've noticed it yourself. Drinks altogether too much. It troubles me. I suppose he'll become reconciled, in time. But the brandy can't help. No. I'm afraid he'll find that troubles can't be drowned in alcohol. On the contrary. Troubles, like drowned corpses, become more bloated and hideous after protracted immersion in fluids."

"I'll be going out to The Croft tomorrow," I volunteered.

"John asked me to speak to Arabella."

"Is that so? He asked me to visit her too, you know. Has some idea she's been drugged or something. That's nonsense, of course, he just can't face the reality; has to seek other reasons to ease the situation. Although I'm sure I'd rather have a daughter—if I had a daughter—seduced by normal sexual processes rather than ruined by narcotics. Anyway, I can't just show up there without being called, of course. She's of age."

I wanted to restore the conversation to Sam Cooper, and said, "This Sam. Would it be your opinion that the man should be committed?"

Plum waved a hand.

"Couldn't say without I'd examined him, you know. Probably couldn't say anyhow, really." He smiled modestly. "I'm just a simple country doctor," he said, with his polished toes glinting. "Of course, if the man is dangerously violent—as he was today—Then again, to hear our good vicar tell it, Mallory himself should be clamped in an asylum. Or a dungeon, more likely. Bound up in chains and guarded by flaming swords."

He chuckled. "A great exponent of the Inquisition is our good vicar. I expect you've heard about the garden party?"

"Something, yes."

"Grimm nearly had a stroke over it." He chuckled again. "Got the gout, too, has Grimm. Mortified by the fact. I've tried to explain that it's just an inflammation caused by metabolic imbalance, but he won't listen. He's certain God gave him gout as penance for his sins, but on the other hand he's equally certain that he's never sinned. Terribly frustrating for the man, a paradox of that magnitude. 'What,' he said, 'what would my flock think, were it known I suffered from the drunkard's disease?'"

I laughed. Then, on sudden impulse, asked, "Where is the vicarage?"

"Why, just up the road here."

"I wonder, would you be so kind as to introduce me to Grimm?"

"Surely. You're not aiming to argue Christianity with him, are you?" he asked, eyes bright, as if he would not be averse to such disputation.

"Certainly not."

Plum drew his watch from his waistcoat, a laborious process. The gold chain reflected in the tips of his shoes. "I have time in hand," he said—I wondered if he meant it literally, for he seemed to be balancing the watch in his palm, perhaps suddenly doubting the weight of gold. "We can stop there now, if you like."

"If it's no imposition."

"Not at all."

And so, uncertain why I was going or what I would ask, I accompanied Plum to the vicarage.

The vicarage was a white house with green gables, and the vicar was a pale man with ginger hair who quite openly welcomed company. I could see how he would pride himself on his garden parties. He ushered us into a small room overlooking the garden and served us sherry, a trifle too sweet. Plum weighed his watch again and exchanged a few civilities. Then, seeming most casual with his eyes twinkling, he informed Grimm that I had come to visit Mallory. The vicar choked on his sherry and turned red, a remarkable process, as if the pigment of his hair were running down to tint his face.

"Am I to assume that Mr. Mallory is a friend or a colleague?" he asked.

"Neither, really. I'm interested in some ancient writings he has."

"Ah." He regarded me more kindly. "Is that so? He actually does have some knowledge of the past, then? I must confess I'd thought the man an utter charlatan."

"He may well be."

Grimm was pleased.

"I've heard you had a disagreement with him?"

"I most certainly did." He looked out the window, probably visualizing the scene. "A most unpleasant man. I had to ask him to depart."

"I was curious about that. I don't mean to pry, but I've argued with Mallory myself, you see."

Grimm saw. He beamed. He leaned toward me like a conspiring anarchist.

"Was he talking about the ancient Egyptian religions?" I inquired.

"Indeed he was. Absolute nonsense. Predates Christianity, of course, so you can't very well blame the old Egyptians for their ignorance. I'm a charitable man, I don't hold their unenlightened and barbaric religion against them. Who am I to judge them? Poor souls, they have long since been judged —severely, no doubt—by God. So, as I say, I suppose it was all right for them—better than no religion at all, eh? Even if they had foul practices. But for a man to champion such beliefs in this day and age, *anno Domini*—well, I ask you! I'm not well versed on the topic, naturally. I'd be interested to hear a rational Christian discuss it."

I had no desire to enter into a theological disquisition, and explained briefly, "Well, their entire existence was a preparation for their deaths. It went deeper than a religion of the afterlife; virtually all their daily procedures were concerned with their ultimate demise. That explains their great concern with mummification and tombs, you see. The Egyptians believed that the soul wandered about after death and that it needed a body to which, from time to time, it could return."

"How remarkable," he said, smiling tolerantly. "Poor children, groping blindly for truth denied them by their age."

I understood why he'd rubbed Mallory across the grain.

"It isn't really so far removed from your—our—beliefs, is it?" I said, causing him to frown. "I mean, an afterlife by any other name—"

"Nonsense."

Plum grinned back and forth between us, ready to be entertained. I overcame the argumentative urge.

"What, specifically, did Mallory claim?" I asked.

"Well, I paid little attention, of course. But there is something—a *Book of the Dead!*"

"Yes."

"What is that, exactly?"

"A set of instructions on how the soul could successfully meet Osiris, the judge of ethical deeds committed in the flesh." I paused, but Grimm looked blank, waiting. "You see, the Egyptians were very materialistic in their concept of death. They simply couldn't conceive of life as other than a physical existence. Therefore they preserved the body and built great fortresses to protect it for eternity. Originally the sarcophagus was inscribed with magic incantations and formulas along with maps of the underworld to guide the deceased. But as the mass of magical knowledge increased, soon they found there was no room left in the sarcophagus and on the scarabs. So all such incantations were gathered together and recorded on rolls of papyrus which could be placed in the tombs. These rolls were the *Book of the Dead* and the *Sarcophagus Texts.*"

"I see," Grimm said. "But to what purpose?"

"Why, for the afterlife. To a people pathetically unable to recognize physical death, it was logical. As they supplied food and furniture and ornaments and even slaves for the use of the dead man, so they provided a ritual by which he could be found virtuous when his deeds were weighed."

"They actually thought a soul needed food?"

I smiled.

"They even included toilets in the tomb."

"Incredible."

"How did these formulas supposedly work?" Plum asked.

"Well, the dead man studied them, and then when he faced Osiris, king of the dead, he was able to recite all the sins he had not committed."

"Had *not* committed?" Plum echoed.

"Barbaric," Grimm muttered.

"Is it? What of the Ten Commandments?"

Grimm stared at me.

"Thou shalt *not* kill, thou shalt *not* covet thy neighbor's wife, and so on. Well, in the *Book of the Dead,* it reads—freely translated—I have known no worthless folk, I have not filched the property of the lowly man, I have not carried off the cakes of the dead, I have not snared geese in the preserves of the gods, and suchlike."

"Both negative confessions, eh?" Plum said.

"Don't know quite what you mean by that, exactly," said Grimm. He frowned ponderously. "One doesn't necessarily have to believe in the Bible word for word—lot of it written by Jews, come to that—but one doesn't necessarily care to have it derided, either. Especially at a garden party, with my flock present. That's what this Mallory chap did. Compared the

Bible unfavorably with the *Book of the Dead*." He sniffed. Plum was grinning.

"So they recited these incantations to appease Osiris, eh?" Plum said.

"To deceive him, actually."

"To deceive him? To deceive him!" Grimm roared.

"Oh, yes."

"These heathens actually believed they could deceive their god? Good heavens! Even a false deity is wiser than a man!"

Plum and I regarded Grimm.

Grimm glared back contentiously. Then he realized what he had said and lowered his face, scowling. Plum was rocking with silent laughter; he concealed a snort with his handkerchief. Grimm muttered, "Well, that's as may be. We are at least rational men here. This Mallory made fouler claims, too. Insults, animadversions. He called Christianity the magic of the Western world. But what was really offensive was when he told the women—why on earth they paid the slightest attention to a visibly mad heretic is beyond me—told them that it wasn't necessary to die, that man had the potential for immortality in the flesh. The flesh, not the spirit. Can you imagine telling them such trash? As if heaven wasn't good enough for anyone!"

"Seems like it ought to be," Plum responded wickedly.

"Exactly. Thank God I had the sense to drive him out when I did. He'd already warped that poor Cunningham girl's mind. Why, who knows, had he stayed he might have caused my entire flock to stray!"

"It was this talk of immortality that impressed Arabella, did it?" I asked, thinking of John's comment that she had left because she feared her life was passing her by.

"Certainly. What else? There is no lust like the lust of the mind. This man tempted her with ideas just as the serpent tempted the innocent Eve with the apple—as Mephisto tempted Faustus with power. We all have our weaknesses.

What beautiful young woman would not be enchanted—bedeviled—by the concept of eternal youth?"

Grimm had a point there.

We left soon afterward.

Once more at the Red Lion, I checked in on John. He was still sleeping, lying on his back. One hand moved spasmodically at the edge of the bed, but he appeared peaceful enough. I retired to my own room and prepared to undertake the translation from the photographic copy. It is strange—or perhaps not strange—how one becomes accustomed to a certain procedure. At the cottage I had my desk at the window, and it didn't seem proper to work in a different position. I pulled the table over to the crooked window overlooking the high street. This was curious also, gazing out over a peaceful English village with the hieroglyphs before me. One felt thrust between two disparate dimensions.

Once, in Egypt, walking along the cliff at dusk, I'd thought myself lost. A sudden wind had risen, and the landscape darkened with sand. The sky directly overhead was clear, but the air around me was enveloped in a cloudy grey turbulence. I'd undergone a moment of panic, thinking I should never find my way back to the camp. Then the panic had subsided. It no longer seemed to matter very much. A sense of eternity fell over me in that timeless wasteland, and I felt a part of the changing sands, at one with ancient Egypt. I sat down and filled my pipe, offering smoke to the powdered sand. Presently a trick of air currents opened a corridor through the storm, disclosing the encampment below me. On all sides the air was black, impenetrable, but looking down that solitary passage I could see clearly. Sir Harold was standing before his tent, a fire had been started. That scene, drawn closer than it was by the optical quirk that revealed it, seemed to have no relation to me. I had the sensation of looking, not through space, but through time; I felt myself of the past, granted a gift of viewing the future. I watched with great interest and objective dispassion, content to remain there in the sands forever. Then the air closed in again and cast me down the ages until, with a click, I was wrenched once more into my niche in time.

Something of that odd sensation came over me now, seated at the crooked window between two worlds. I mused over the feeling for a while, then lighted my pipe and prepared to work. The sky had begun to cloud over, and soft diffused light lay shadowless on the table. I arranged my papers and loosened my necktie. Coots left the Red Lion, and Constable Chive sauntered down the street. They stopped to exchange a few words, and Coots was grinning, two antagonists in a moment of armistice.

The translation wasn't particularly difficult, although I saw why Mallory, with his limited learning, had not been able to manage it. He likely was versed only in a single period, and language evolves through the long ages. The great duration of the Egyptian Empire extended over many such modifications in the symbolism of the script, and the hieroglyphs before me were, to the more common examples, as Middle English is to modern English. As the translation began to emerge, I wondered why Mallory had been concerned that I kept it confidential. There was nothing new or startling in the text, yet it was the content which interested him. After several hours of labor the translation was complete. It was a description of the embalming process, written by a physician—or priest, the two were synonymous in that time when physical death was unimaginable—and the methods described were similar to those already known about the art of mummification.

Completed, the translation read:

A crooked piece of iron, of design suited to the deed, was inserted up the nostrils and hooked into the brain. The brain was then drawn out through the nose. Next, using a sharpened Ethiopian stone, a cut was made along the flank and the intestines were extracted and, as is fitting, were purified with palm wine and pounded spices. The body cavity was filled with finely powdered myrrh, cinnamon, and spices but for frankincense which was not used. It was then sewn up again, and placed in natron for seventy days. It must be left no longer. When the seventy days have ended, the body must be washed carefully and bound in strips of fine linen, smeared with gum. The relatives will then have fashioned a wooden coffin to fit the body, and shutting the man up in this coffin, they will place it upright in the sepulchral chamber which will be its home. Above the ground will be made a brickwork structure, gaily painted and adorned to suggest the palace of the man in this life and by which his wandering soul will know and recognize the place and by which he will not by error enter into the body of another man, which blunder would cause calamity in his world.

That was all.

I reviewed the translation and entered several minor emendations before I was satisfied, then wondered if Mallory would be pleased or if he had expected more of the content. I was looking forward to examining the tablet itself, for the translation made it clear that it was old; that it antedated the royal pyramids which came to replace the brick simulation of the deceased man's home. No matter what curious theories Mallory entertained, or how mistakenly he assigned his values, he obviously had come to possess some treasures of the past.

I stood and stretched.

A knock sounded at the door.

I opened it.

"Good evening, sir," Inspector Peal announced in funereal tones.

Peal entered my quarters, a big beefy man with a rather wrinkled suit. "What can I do for you, Inspector?" I asked. He didn't immediately reply, but looked around the room and ambled over to the window, where he stood silently contemplating my papers while rubbing the back of his neck. He picked up my translation and glanced at it.

"Gruesome sort of business, wasn't it?"

"Oh, no worse than present-day funerals, I daresay."

"Yes, yes. Probably right there. When you come to think of it, I guess maybe I'd rather be stuffed full of spices than pumped full of formaldehyde." He smiled and put the paper down. "This, I take it, is the work you're doing for Mr. Mallory?"

"I'm doing nothing for Mallory," I replied. "I'm doing it for myself. But, yes, that's a translation of one of his clay tablets."

"Valuable?"

"Rather. I haven't seen it. This translation was made from a copy."

"Um. He does have these objects, though?"

"Certainly."

"I was under the impression that you'd be staying at his house."

"I shall be. Apparently he wasn't ready for me."

"But you are going out there?"

I nodded.

Peal walked over to the bed, then came back.

"Mr. Ashley, this is all rather irregular, but I intend to ask your help." I raised my eyebrows as he continued, "I'd like you to look around The Croft while you're there and report to me later."

"Look around? For what?"

"I don't know."

"A rather imprecise request."

"I realize that, sir. But it's just possible you might notice something, well, out of the usual."

"He's an unusual fellow."

"I take it you have no fondness for him?"

"I have no desire for playing the spy, either."

Peal appeared pained.

"Why not obtain a search warrant and look for yourself? I don't even know what you're looking for."

"We really have no reason to apply for a warrant. Just a few coincidences. And a formal search—believe me, sir, it would be better to avoid that."

"More convenient for you, you mean?"

"Better in all ways."

"Do you actually suspect Mallory?"

"No, sir, I don't," he said, but there was a slight hesitation before his reply. He stared at me, waiting for my response. I thought for several moments.

"If I'm going to spy on the man, I feel entitled to know your reasons, Inspector."

"Curiosity? Or justification?"

"Both, I suppose."

"Um. Not particularly ethical, but I guess there's no harm in it. You'll keep this confidential, of course?"

"Of course."

"Well, sit down."

I sat at the table. Peal drew up another chair and crossed his legs. His shoes were muddy. "There isn't much, actually. A set of minor coincidences, a couple of facts that don't quite jibe. You don't mind if I smoke? Right. Well, first off, the initial murder victim had been a houseguest at The Croft."

"Mallory admitted that."

"Did he? Yes, he told us as much. Snow, the man's name was. Apparently a well-known brain surgeon. Once we'd identified the body we had to trace him back to London before we'd any idea what he was doing down here. No one in the village knew him or had seen him. We learned from his office that he'd been at Mallory's for several weeks."

"Weeks?"

Peal glanced up sharply.

"Yes, several weeks," he repeated. "Nothing suspicious about that. But London gave us to believe that Snow had been here to see about some new developments or methods related to brain surgery. We assumed that Mallory was a doctor or scientist. However, when we checked this out at The Croft, Mallory claimed that Snow had come to examine a man—his servant—who'd suffered some brain damage in an accident. Is that in accord with what he told you?"

"It is. I know the man. Sam Cooper. I knew him before the accident as well, and can testify that he certainly has been injured."

"Yes, we ascertained that," Peal nodded. "But that brings us to the first, well, inconsistency. If Snow were to make a proper examination, he'd have needed equipment—x-ray machine, surgery, whatever. And obviously, Mallory not being a doctor, he could not have found that equipment at The Croft. It is possible that he came merely to make a preliminary examination, of course—although his office maintains that Snow never worked in that way—but if that were the case, the examination would have taken only a day or two at the most, after which he'd have to have the patient brought to London. Why then did he remain for several weeks?"

"I've no idea."

"Nor had we. Apparently Snow was a very thorough and conscientious man. He would hardly have been satisfied with less than a full examination. Nor had he brought any of his portable equipment with him." Peal frowned and regarded me intently. "This bothered me. I went back to Mallory's and put the question to him. He didn't seem surprised at all, and told me that Snow and he were friends; that Snow had come on a friendly visit and had examined Sam Cooper merely as a favor to Mallory. I asked why he'd not told us that in the first place, and he said it hadn't seemed important. Probably didn't, to him. Somehow, though, I wasn't satisfied with this. Why would Snow have let his office think he was on a business trip? Oh, perhaps he wanted to get away for a while, take a holiday, you know, without anyone realizing he was relaxing. Quite likely. Men, especially important, conscientious men, get that way. They get the idea that it's wrong to neglect their work. Don't know why." The inspector grinned and assumed a diffident expression. "I go to Torquay every year, myself. Take the wife. Never think about work at all for a fortnight. That's as may be.

"Still, a few aspects didn't seem to fit into place. Snow's wife, for instance, had never heard Snow mention Mallory. Now that's odd—old friends and all—friendly enough for a two-week visit. Well, it gave me to consider. There are quite logical explanations, of course. Who knows? Snow might have had a woman with him, something like that. Maybe Mallory was in the habit of fixing him up with a girl from time to time. Nothing much wrong with that. I've seen worse. Seen it happen right in Torquay, even. Men you'd never dream of as philanderers, all of a sudden they turn up with some young doxy or other, drinking and dancing and God knows what. Well, I'm not trying to make a point of morality over this, just mention it as a possibility. We may never know—"

He paused. I said, "Is that all?"

"Not quite. Snow's body, as you may know, was found not far from The Croft. Mallory claims that Snow had left, intending to walk to the train station in the village here. Said he offered to drive him in, but that it was a fine day and Snow preferred to get the exercise. Maybe so. But just on the odd chance I had that checked with Snow's wife. She told us that her husband never walked. Had a right hatred of walking, in fact. Apparently he used to maintain that walking and exercise was only fit behavior for heart surgeons and general practitioners, and that brain surgeons were above such nonsense. Well, on holiday maybe he was different. Maybe." He shook his head doubtfully, and then continued, "We haven't found his suitcase yet, however. Figure the killer must've made off with it. That's strange, it didn't look as if the motive was robbery, and Snow had money in his pockets. Why would the killer have stolen a suitcase and left money? Just another piece that doesn't quite fit. Then this second murder occurs. Lad killed close by The Croft; actually on his way there, in fact. Well, sir, you can see how these minor inconsistencies begin to add up."

I cleared my throat. "Surely just coincidence."

"Oh, no doubt."

"What reason could Mallory have to kill Snow?"

"What reason did Snow have, really, to come here?"

"Hm. Well, leave Snow out of it. Mallory could certainly have had no reason to kill the boy."

"No. Unless," Peal shifted uneasily in his chair, "this isn't an official theory, but suppose Mallory—or anyone, for that matter—killed Snow for some definite reason. Then he got the wind up; was afraid that our investigations would uncover his motive. Might he not decide to obscure the issue, to make it appear the work of a madman, motiveless, by killing again?"

"That's rather farfetched."

"Yes, as I said, not an official theory."

"I still don't know what I'm supposed to be looking for at The Croft?"

"No, I don't suppose you do. It's just that you might come upon something accidentally. For instance, now that you know the story—suppose you were to find Snow's suitcase?"

"I see," I replied, realizing for the first time that Mallory actually was a genuine suspect.

"You will keep your eyes open, then, sir?" Peal asked, standing up.

"Yes, all right."

"I appreciate it. In a case like this, we have to look at all the possibilities. What's been done is bad enough. Any way we can prevent another murder—"

He moved heavily toward the door; I rose to usher him out, but he turned back.

"Oh, and I'd advise you to be careful."

"Careful? Do you think I'm in danger?"

"With a madman, sir, everyone is in danger. After all, Snow was a houseguest at The Croft, just as you will be. And the Brooke lad was headed there, just as you."

"Oh, I shall be all right."

A trace of annoyance passed over Peal's face.

"Overconfidence doesn't do, Ashley," he said. "There are certain aspects to these murders—things so gruesome that we've thus far kept them quiet, to avoid panic. But you had best not be incautious. No solitary walks, nothing like that. No doubt you think yourself fit and able to defend yourself. No doubt Snow felt the same way. But this madman is inordinately powerful. Preternaturally so, in fact." Peal was staring solemnly at me. "The bodies were mutilated in a degree —Ashley, it looked more like the work of a wild beast than a man. The doctor had never seen anything like it. The pure frenzy of the attack—The killer didn't cease until long after the victim was dead. It was as if murder wasn't enough, as if he wanted to utterly destroy the body. And Ashley, the bones were crushed and the flesh torn—by human teeth."

Then he went out.

6

I retired early that evening and slept well enough, mercifully without dreams. Dawn arrived serene and clear, a burnished saffron glow on the eastern rim. I dressed and went down to the breakfast room, intending to telephone Mallory after I had eaten, but as I sat in those cheerful surroundings with the early morning sunlight shimmering in the yellow curtains, I instead determined to walk out to The Croft. It was only two or three miles, an hour's jaunt at the most, and I told myself I needed the exercise. But was that the reason? Or had my conversation with Peal induced me to behave like an investigator? Did I wish to trace the path on which my telegram had sent the messenger to his ghastly death? Perhaps.

I sought out Mabel, settled for my second night's lodging, and secured specific directions to The Croft; went up to look in on John, who watched me with quiet eyes and made no attempt to move his shattered jaw; and finally repaired to my room and packed my valise. As I lifted it, the weight struck a response. I had brought little enough, but the suitcase would be bothersome to carry along, and moreover it occurred to me that I might just as well arrive at Mallory's without luggage. God knew what things would be like there. If I were to leave my suitcase at the Red Lion, I would have a ready excuse for early departure. Resolved upon this, I opened the case again and put my toothbrush into my pocket, then took the case down and arranged to leave it with Mabel. She was amenable enough, hoping for further custom. She accompanied me to the door, and as I stepped into the street, said, "Don't let the monster get you now, Mr. Ashley." I saw that she had been converted to Coots's thinking.

Fleecy clouds were pulling apart in patterns against a cerulean sky, above venerable oak trees, dividing like woolly amoebas in their eternal solitude. Clouds, like the single-celled stuff of life, were immortal, I thought; it is only awareness of death that curses man with mortality. I walked along a narrow path with hedgerows on one side and rolling fields on the other. It was a gentle region, one known to young Brooke all his life, and an incongruous setting in which to perish by violence. I wondered if I'd know the spot when I came to it. Perhaps there would be visible signs, the undergrowth torn up, the ground gorged by drinking blood, chalk marks made by the police to describe the position of the body; perhaps I would sense the scene instinctively, by a chill of the flesh, a dim cry in my ears. Was it more terrible to die in such an unlikely locale, or was it a peaceful landscape to lay a corpse, mild and pretty, where the dead body could take root and sprout new life from its own decay, regenerated by the fertility of its spilled fluids?

I wanted to smoke and played a game with myself, seeing how far I could progress before yielding to the urge. It was a charade in which I sometimes indulged on walks by my cottage, where the landmarks were well known, but here on a strange path I found new dimensions added, new rules and unexpected goals. Just one more tree, I told myself; no, not that one, the larger one ahead; and then, just to that pillar of rock, that was easy enough, we'll just attempt to make it as far as that fence ahead, and all the while thinking how curious it was that clean fresh air invariably instills the desire for tobacco. Paradoxes known to man, I mused, and patted my pocket to assure myself that my pipe was waiting there; taking strength from the assurance to walk another hundred yards without surrendering to the temptation. I was making good progress, my legs felt light and strong, I gazed about at the countryside and down at the dusty path where my long shadow ran out before me as if stamped from the earth. Presently I heard an automobile in the distance, coming from behind. It drew closer, sound waves compressing. I didn't look back, but as it closed I stepped to the side to let it pass. Instead, the vehicle drew up beside me. It was a police car. The driver was uniformed. Inspector Peal, beside him, nodded out at me.

"On your way to The Croft?" he asked.

"Yes."

"Give you a lift?"

I hesitated, content to walk.

"I'm going near there. Looks like we might have our first break." He knew that would interest me. I clambered into the back seat. Exercise abandoned, I gave up the game and began filling my pipe. The car started up smoothly. Peal offered nothing further.

"What has happened?" I asked.

"Looks like we may have a couple people who saw the killer," he said. "Group of vagabonds camped out here. Chive had an idea they might've seen something—says they don't miss much—and it turns out it was a pretty good idea at that. Looks like they saw the killer either just before, or just after, he did the Brooke lad in."

"How can you know it was he?"

"Well, can't, really. But whoever they saw scared hell out of them, so we know at least he looked strange. They're a superstitious lot, and suspicious, too, and if they were more frightened by this character than they are by Constable Chive, well, he must've looked pretty wild. That could be an advantage, too. If he looks normal, what the hell. But if we can get a description that sets him apart, then we have something to work on."

"But if they didn't actually see him kill the boy—"

Peal snorted.

"Ah, we'd never get them into court to testify, even if they did. They'd just hitch up their wagons and move on. Outside our legal system, they are. Deny everything. Hard to even identify them as witnesses. But that's not my worry, I just want to find this guy before he kills again."

We drove on.

Chive was standing beside a call box, his bicycle leaning against a rough hewn fence. We drew up beside him, and he approached the car, touching his helmet.

" 'Fraid you'll have to leave the car here," he said. "It's not far."

"You manage from here?" Peal asked me.

"May I come with you?"

Peal looked at me and shrugged.

"Don't see why not."

The driver remained with the car, and Chive led us through the fence and out across the field. The landscape extended in a profusion of daisy-bedizened verdure, while a line of rocky tors loomed starkly on the horizon. Chive was chattering, "You must understand, sir, these are difficult people. They have no faith in legal justice. Not easy to get a word out of them. You see, they have no sense of innocence, not to mention guilt. Suspicious. As far as they know, seein' a murderer is just as great a crime as committing a murder."

"But did they admit seeing someone?" the inspector asked.

"Yes, sir, they did. But as for judging the truth of their words—why, they no more know what truth is than attempt to tell it."

"Hm. Can we offer them something? Tobacco? A few bob?"

"Wouldn't advise it. They see the chance for gain, why they'd say whatever they thought you wanted to hear."

"Just what did they tell you?"

"I'd rather, if it's all right, sir, have them repeat it to you."

Peal looked at him.

"What's got you upset, Chive?" he asked.

"Well, sir—they think it was a werewolf."

"Oh," replied Peal, and we walked on.

The earth was soft underfoot, sucking at my boots as if to draw me down into the ground, a vast grave yearning for a tenant. As we neared the top of the rise I detected the gypsy camp below us, beside a narrow stream. The wagons were drawn up by a small copse. They were brightly painted and gaily trimmed and had huge wooden wheels. The horses grazed off to one side; large patient brutes with great shaggy feet. As we approached I noticed that a small dark man and a woman in a bright shawl were sitting on the steps of the first wagon. No one else was in sight, although I sensed eyes in the other wagons. Both figures were smoking stubby black pipes; the man looked sullen, the woman nervous.

"Mind the dog," Chive cautioned.

"What?" said Peal, and as he spoke a buckskin blur rushed at him from beside the wagon. Peal stepped back very quickly, colliding with me. I had a flashing glimpse of Chive's unintentional grin. Something clanked, and the dog's charge was arrested a scant yard from our legs.

"He's chained, sir," Chive reported belatedly.

"What in hell is that?" asked Peal.

"Pit bull terrier, sir."

The brute, straining on a heavy length of chain, thundered with muscle. It made no sound whatsoever: the warning lay in its eyes, malevolent yellow orbs glowering upon us. The creature was not very tall, though its legs bowed around the mightiest chest I have ever seen on a dog. The choke collar cut into its throat, unnoticed, as it strained to ravage us. The man on the wagon was amused, although still sullen. He waited for a few moments before he called back the bull terrier. It obeyed instantly, but reluctantly, its none-too-gracious retreat attended by an obbligato of menacing snarls. Its fangs were obtrusive ivory triangles in that slavering wedge of a jaw.

"Some dog," Peal observed.

"Pit bull, sir," Chive reiterated, somewhat grimly. "Don't expect you see many of them up at London."

"We do not."

"They use them to fight."

"Fight what?"

"Well, anything, really. But mostly they fight other pit bulls. It's a sort of sport among these people. Wagering and all. Not legal, of course. But hard to catch 'em at it. I've been on the lookout."

"Worse things than dog fights," Peal said.

"Yes, sir. They are bred to it."

The bull terrier had assumed a couchant posture beside the wagon, not curling as dogs do but down on its belly with its paws extended fore and aft because of the width of that massive block of body. It continued to scrutinize us with watchful golden eyes. Peal, walking gingerly, moved up to the wagon.

"This is Inspector Peal," Chive announced. "He'd like you to tell him as you told me, Mr. Smith."

"Already told it once," Smith said.

"Yes, if you'll just repeat it."

"You forgot it, eh?"

"Just cooperate," Peal said harshly.

The dog drew back its lips.

"Quiet, Job," Smith said. He looked up at Peal. "I call him Job. That's from the Holy Book. I call him that because he has great patience. Once he closes his teeth in another living creature, he will never relent until that creature has ceased to live."

"It's a fine dog," Peal observed.

"Dumb brute. Don't know but to bite. Just as soon take the leg off a policeman as not."

"Yes, I can imagine. Well now, if you'll be kind enough to tell me about this stranger you saw?"

"Had to tell about the dog first."

Peal appeared puzzled.

"That's right, isn't it?" Smith asked Chive.

"That's right, sir," Chive agreed.

"What's the connection?"

Smith looked at the constable.

"Well, sir," said Chive, "it appears as how this dog was terrified by the stranger."

Peal offered cigarettes to the couple. They both accepted one, carefully banking their pipes for later. After they were smoking, Peal inquired, "So you saw this man—what? Three nights ago, right?"

"Weren't no man."

"Well, whatever."

"That's right, three nights past."

"Just tell me how you saw him and what he looked like."

"I didn't do nothing wrong?"

"No, not at all."

"Can't get in any trouble for seeing him?"

"No."

Smith puffed, squinting in the smoke. Peal waited, one eye on Job. The dog returned an expression of undeviating animosity. His master cleared his throat: "It was like this. I was throwing sticks for Job. That is because I have to exercise him or he gets fat. Not lazy, but fat. So, what I do, I release his chain from the wagon but keep it around his neck. That way, when he runs, he drags the heavy chain behind him and that is good exercise for his chest and legs. But it is hard for me, because each time I have to fetch a new stick. That is because when Job bites a stick, it breaks. Every time, snap, snap. His jaws are very strong."

"Go on," Peal encouraged.

"I threw these sticks as far as I could, down toward the stream. It was just coming on nighttime with lots of shadows. That was why I didn't notice the creature come out from the trees and across the stream. I threw another stick, Job took after it. It was turning around in the air and I was watching it, and then it hit the ground right at this creature's feet." Smith paused a moment and regarded his audience earnestly. "Gave me a surprise, I'd not been aware of him. But, you see, I thought it to be a man. I was afraid that Job would savage him, and I jumped up to run after him. The creature didn't seem to notice the stick, though it fell right at his feet. He just stood there in the shadows. Job charged up low, dragging the chain, and I came hustling up behind him, thinking that if Job had his leg off there'd be grievous trouble.

"Then Job stopped.

"He just stopped dead in front of the creature and lowered his back. Not like he was about to spring, but like he was struck to the ground. Job has never feared anything living, but he feared this creature. I came to a stop then too, and looked at the creature's face. He was just staring off into the distance. Job whined like a lapdog. Then the creature looked down at him. He just sort of dropped his head, like his neck was broken, like a hanged man on a rope. There was something horrible about it. Job howled and spun right around and came running back with his tail down and his ears back. Ran right past me. I just stood there. The creature looked up at me, slow this time. I looked right at his face. Wasn't human. Don't know what it was, but it wasn't human. I turned and ran back to get my shotgun. Job was under the wagon whimpering. I looked back, but the creature was just standing there, as if to make up its mind whether to come after me. Then it turned and moved off into the trees. Most horrible thing I ever saw."

Smith shuddered and lapsed into silence. The woman had paled. Peal waited a moment, then asked, "Can you describe him?"

"Big. It was dark. White face, big white eyes. Not hairy, like a werewolf, but not human, neither."

"Anything else about him? Any scars? How was he dressed?"
Smith shook his head.

"You must have noticed more than that."

"Just big. Big white eyes."

Peal sighed and glanced at Chive. The constable shrugged.

"Guess I better have a look down by the stream. There might be some footprints. Probably just some poacher."

"It did scare the dog, sir," Chive said.

"Hm. Well, the dog scared me, so that's square."

Peal, obviously not satisfied with what he had learned, walked toward the water. Chive put one foot on the step.

"What's this about a shotgun, then?" he asked.

Smith didn't understand.

"Wouldn't have been no good, anyhow," the gypsy mumbled. "You'd need a silver bullet."

"Were you aware you needed a permit to possess a gun?" Chive asked. Smith frowned, his eyes becoming sullen once more. It was easy enough to see why these people resented authority. I left the camp and headed back for the road.

The sky appeared to have arched its back as the morning wore on, and the clouds were higher and thinner, spread across a vaulted firmament with the sunlight filtering through them like a fan. The light seemed to have left its warmth in the clouds; it was colder and the shadows less distinct. I looked back from the incline. Peal was bending down by the stream and Chive was standing over Smith, hands clasped behind his back. The gypsy was gesticulating. His dog had cocked its head, listening with those crudely cropped ears, scarred body taut.

It was impossible to imagine that fierce brute terrified at the mere sight of a strange man. Yet I didn't think Smith was lying. He had nothing to gain by fabricating such a tale and, furthermore, had seemed disturbed merely by recalling the incident. That was another inconsistency for Peal; I could only hope that a pattern emerged before the killer struck again. As for the theories that were beginning to occur to me, well, they were just that—theories, not yet ready to be accorded affirmative utterance.

I rejoined the road some distance from where the police car waited at the call box. The driver was leaning against the fender, smoking a cigarette. I proceeded along the road and, rounding the next turn, closer than I had thought to the vagabond camp, beheld Mallory's house. It was a grim grey structure surmounted by steep tile-hung gables, the sort of residence that would have seemed more appropriate over-looking a rocky seacoast than commanding gentle fields. The dwelling was set back from the road and surrounded by a labyrinth of grey stone fences, seemingly erected at random. A great many of the stones had fallen, and here and there the fences had sunk down in the moist earth.

The house itself was in no better repair. The creeper-clad west wall had buckled outward slightly and the dilapidated roof listed alarmingly, while the chimney, like the painting in my room at the Red Lion, remained perfectly upright. I paused at the foot of the weed-engulfed drive. The sunlight was striking down on all sides, but by some trick of refraction the structure was ensconced in shadow; it seemed farther away than the light. I understood why Coots had described it as an "eerie old place" and could well imagine how it appeared in darkness with the latticed windows lighted.

The ideal setting for a spy, I thought, not relishing the dual purpose of my visit.

The night before it had seemed only logical to agree to assist Peal in any way I might, but now with the house before me, I felt rather treacherous. Mallory was hardly an appealing character, but he had never harmed me. The man had, in fact, trusted me to a degree, and he deserved more than deceit. This troubled me. I endeavored to rationalize by assuring myself that if he was innocent I could do him no wrong, and if, on the unlikely prospect, he concealed some dark guilt, he then had forfeited all claims to my loyalty. But such soul-searching casuistry is merely an expedient balm to the conscience. My exquisite philosophical ruminations regarding whether the end justified the means could only be properly considered *a posteriori,* in retrospect.

Turning up the drive, I thus was uncomfortable. I felt dishonest; that I should not be approaching openly from the front of the house but should come cloaked in night like an agent dropped into occupied territory, or in disguise like some latter-day sultan skulking through the maze of Baghdad. It was all academic, I told myself; Mallory could not possibly be responsible for the murders. I strode along the crumbling fence and up to the shadowy weather-stained facade.

Mallory's car was parked beside the house, situated between a stone outbuilding in which the roof had collapsed and a woodpile on which an axe was standing, the blade buried in a log. I wondered if Mallory chopped his own wood or hired local help, or perhaps allotted such tasks to Sam Cooper. I wouldn't have cared to trust Sam, in his deranged state, with an axe. The front steps were stone, the door was heavy oak with a brass knocker in need of polish. When I raised the knocker it groaned. I let it drop against the plate. The rusty hinge was louder than the rap of contact. I waited. After a few moments there were sounds within.

Arabella Cunningham opened the door.

A pretty child, she had become a striking woman, with dark eyes, dark hair, a delicate bone structure. She smiled, recognizing me.

"Hello, Thomas," she greeted.

"Arabella. Didn't expect you'd remember me."

"Lucian told me you'd be coming. A friend of my father's, he said." She paused, one hand on the door. "I'd have known you anyway." She stepped back and I entered. She closed the door behind us. "How is father?"

"Well enough. You heard what happened?"

She nodded slowly, biting her lower lip.

"Was it father's fault?"

"Well, he acted first—"

"Lucian said he'd been drinking?"

With malice, I wondered, or merely with a shrewd mind for the facts, not considering that this was the man's daughter? One or the other, I thought. Mallory was no man to seek to justify himself. Still, it seemed hardly necessary to tell her that.

I shrugged. "He's worried about you."

"Yes. He's all right, though?"

"His jaw is broken."

Arabella winced.

"I can't imagine what got into Sam," she said slowly. "He was so docile at first—until a week or so ago—then he changed abruptly. I suppose one must expect irrational behavior in these cases."

"Shouldn't he be properly cared for? Looked after by competent people?"

"An asylum? That sounds so grim."

"This whole place is rather grim," I noted, glancing over the mildewed oaken paneling and dingy black-and-white tiles in the once-handsome hallway.

She surprised me by laughing.

"It is rather, isn't it?"

"I—John wonders if you are well?"

Again she surprised me, hesitating, as though the question required contemplation. She said nothing. I continued lamely, "I'm afraid I've rather pried into your affairs. Unintentionally. In a village like Farriers Bar—"

"Oh, the vicar's garden party," she said.

"Are you sure this is the best place for you, Arabella?"

"Why, not at all."

I blinked.

"I shan't be staying long," she told me.

"I'd thought—"

"You didn't believe the local gossip, surely, Thomas?"

She seemed amused.

I felt embarrassed.

"I'm not living with Lucian, you know," she proclaimed with an insouciant toss of her burnished brunet hair. "I mean —not that way. We aren't lovers."

I believed her.

"I'm afraid your father doesn't realize that."

Her eyes widened. They were large splendid eyes.

"Why, I explained that to him."

I nodded.

"Didn't he believe me?"

"Well, I—perhaps you weren't very emphatic?"

"Emphatic? Well, no. I mean—it just seemed incredible he should think that. I suppose I just brushed it aside because it was so far from the truth. Lucian is a fascinating man, but hardly the type one falls in love with."

"I'm glad. None of my business, of course, but nevertheless I'm glad for John's sake. You must admit, the way you came out here, the way you met—"

"Do you know," she interposed, lowering her voice, "I haven't been able to figure out myself why I did that. It was a remarkable way to behave, wasn't it? Not at all in character. Sometimes I wonder if he didn't hypnotize me."

I looked at her.

"Oh, not literally. I mean—he charmed me, dazzled me, with the scope of his mind. I'd never met anyone like him before. And there in the drab setting of the garden party— by contrast, as it were. I suppose I wanted to shock all those horrid people, cause them to choke on their tea." She laughed. "But, as you can see, I'm perfectly well. I'm helping Lucian care for Sam. And with his experiments—"

"Experiments? A strange term to describe the study of an ancient civilization."

"Well, studies, then."

"Surely you aren't qualified for that?"

She glanced over her shoulder.

"Oh, I'm just an errand boy, really," she murmured.

Then Mallory entered the hall.

Raising an avalanche of eyebrows above the caverns of his eyes, my host advanced with his hand extended.

"I'd expected you to ring me," he greeted.

"I walked out."

"Ah."

"Thought I'd tempt the fates."

"How's that?"

"Like Snow," I said. "Risking the walk instead of accepting your offer to drive me." I smiled. Mallory smiled too, while Arabella looked back and forth between us.

"Well, I've a room ready for you now, at any rate. Have you no luggage?"

"I retained my room at the Red Lion."

This seemed to disturb Mallory. Perhaps he was regretting his former inhospitality. "But that wasn't necessary," he chided. "No matter. We can always send for it. Tell me, were you able to complete the translation?"

I handed him the manila envelope containing the photocopy and my own transcription. He surprised me by putting it in his pocket without glancing at the contents.

"Will you show Ashley to his room?" he asked Arabella. He turned to me. "As soon as you get settled in I'll take you to my workroom. You're prepared to start?"

I nodded. "I'd rather expected you to ask about John Cunningham."

"Oh. Yes. How is he?"

"His jaw is broken."

"Um. Too bad."

Arabella frowned.

"How is Sam?" I asked.

"Oh, he's quite calmed down."

"As I mentioned to Arabella, it seems he should have proper care."

Mallory gestured the suggestion aside.

"You really mustn't trouble yourself over that," he said. "Sam is perfectly all right unless something agitates him."

"Just so I don't attack you, eh?"

Smiling, Mallory said, "You wouldn't do that."

I regarded him wryly for a moment, and then Arabella conducted me to my room.

After protesting that he hadn't readied a room for me, Mallory seemed to have expended little enough effort. The chamber was musty, and the wallpaper blotched with dampness. I sat on the four-poster bed and was enveloped in a pungent mantle of dust. It occurred to me that a bedroom must have been in use while Snow was staying here, and I wondered why Mallory hadn't given me that one; why he had maintained the feeble pretense of preparing accommodation. Surely not a matter of good taste? Not wishing to assign me the same quarters that had housed a dead man? No, Mallory would entertain no such sensibilities. And whatever duties Arabella might or might not have around the house, she obviously had done nothing to enhance the appointments of this room. Well, she was not a chambermaid. Nor did I care much for physical amenities and, furthermore, did not intend to remain longer than necessary. I had no desire to be comfortable in Lucian Mallory's dreary abode.

The bathroom was located at the end of the hall, and, en route to wash up, I passed several closed doors. Obligated to Peal, I felt I should inspect those rooms, but accepting Mallory's hospitality, such as it was, I became reluctant. Then, too, I'd no desire to be caught opening doors and appearing ridiculous, and decided to postpone the investigation until later. It in any case seemed rather pointless: Mallory was no fool, and if he were responsible for Snow's death he would surely have had the sense to dispose of the man's belongings. Or would he? He was not a criminal, and perhaps his mind would not operate in an evasive manner; perhaps it wouldn't have occurred to him that there was necessity to elude the law; that he could not possibly come under suspicion. I should undertake the investigation, I told myself, if only to be able to report to Peal that I had; if only to allay his suspicions. It was not as though I would be trying to prove Mallory guilty; I should rather be proving his innocence. Or so I reasoned. The decision was taken from me, however, for when I returned to the hall, Mallory was waiting outside my room.

"Shall we go down to the workroom?" he asked.

"All right. You've reviewed my translation?"

"I have."

He didn't seem impressed.

"Was it satisfactory?"

"Oh, yes. It was nothing new, of course; I knew that. New by way of content, I meant. But I'm quite satisfied with your competence."

"Which you'd doubted?"

We were descending the main staircase past a ghastly alabaster representation of a nude Victorian nymph.

"Why no, not doubted. But it's just as well to make certain, eh? Reputations are not always grounded on ability. Take Sir Harold Gregory, for instance. A good example, especially since you were working with him—"

"Quite understandable," I replied coldly. It was understandable, too, but Mallory's manner made it irritating. Perhaps he intended it so, deliberately deploying his personality as if being abrasive were a virtue, an art form; as if men, like precious stones, should not yield their sharp edges when they are polished; like cutting tools, can still inflict a wound though the steel is smooth. To my discredit, I found myself hoping his Egyptian findings would prove of little value.

His workroom was at the rear of the house, in a wing apparently older than the facade and built lower into the ground. We proceeded through a dark corridor, Mallory moving ahead of me. He strode past a closed compartment. As I followed, I glanced at it and was surprised to see the entrance fastened by a massive crossbar on the outside. The bar and the fittings were both new, although the method was ancient, and I wondered what reason there could be for locking the door in this manner. Obviously not to secure whatever was kept within, for anyone could lift the bar and enter from the corridor. It occurred to me that the door must open to the exterior of the house, yet that seemed unlikely unless there were a courtyard in the middle of the building. I had paused, and Mallory glanced back. He saw my interest in the door.

"Yes," he nodded. "Those are Sam's quarters." He said this as if to forestall my questioning.

"You keep him locked in?"

"I thought it advisable, after yesterday's incident—"

"But, my God, he's a human being."

Mallory smiled.

"No doubt of that," he said.

"You can't keep him caged like an animal!"

"I can't? But you see, I do. You have a habit of leaping to indefensible conclusions, Ashley."

"I meant, you shouldn't."

"Ah. In his present condition, he's no more than an animal, you know. Less, perhaps, in some ways. And more, too. He has no objections."

"You asked him, I suppose?"

"Believe me, it's better this way. Of course—" He raised his eyebrows. "If you would prefer to have him wandering about the house—why, lift the bar, by all means. Sam won't harm me."

"For Lord's sake, Mallory. He just sits in there all day, a prisoner?"

"Not a prisoner. That implies a sentence, a definite duration. You know nothing of time. Nor does Sam. He does not suffer. Not at all. All forms of suffering are caused by chemical imbalances and glandular secretions, and Sam, because of the extent of his brain damage, can feel none of those emotions. Fortunate, in a way."

I shook my head in disbelief. "You're an incredible man, Mallory."

"Yes, I am rather, aren't I?"

"And insufferable."

"To you? Or to Sam? Why be antagonistic, Ashley. Go ahead, if you will. Lift the bar. Open the door. Sam will come out to see you."

Mallory was smiling coldly. His eyes were gathering twin points of light.

"Yes," he sneered. "Sam will come out."

I had a searing vision of Sam's face, horribly contorted, as he crouched over John and myself; as he drew me effortlessly toward his gaping jaws. No, I was not going to open that door. Mallory knew as much. It was satisfaction which caused him to smile. I turned from the door and followed him to his workroom.

It was a curious sanctum, to say the least, this workroom of Mallory's. He ushered me in with a gesture, and standing just inside the door, I looked about in amazement. A large chamber with stone walls, hung with faded tapestries and set with high narrow windows, it resembled nothing so much as an underground burial vault. Yet remarkable though the room might be, it was the contents that I found singular. Mallory had collected a vast hoard of objects and artifacts which were scattered about without any semblance of order; strewn at random on tables and shelves and packing crates. It was as if, unable to define the purpose of this room, he had fashioned a contrived combination of museum, storehouse, and laboratory; unable to isolate his own interests, he spent his days bolting back and forth from shelf to shelf amid the confusion.

Mallory was peering at me, gauging my impressions, as

I regarded the room. And I found it hard to gauge my own impressions, to decide if this were the study of a scholar or the armamentarium of a madman. There were hundreds of relics from Egypt and Haiti, and some of these were no more than the souvenirs one might purchase in any bazaar or market. Mallory obviously was not discriminating. There were angular figurines of stone and wood, stalking deities and squat gods, twisted serpents and graceful birds, Horus and Isis in worthless representations, modern plaster casts made from ancient molds, a set of orange and black voodoo drums of goatskin, a necklace of crocodile teeth. These things were palpably tasteless and without artistic merit.

Yet amid this rubbish, jumbled together as though he knew not the difference, I began to perceive other objects, venerable and valuable. One by one they emerged phoenixlike from the rubble: I gazed upon an amulet of lapis lazuli, a beetle-shaped scarab inscribed with mystic incantations, clay tablets of indeterminate age, talismans from the Nile. There was a complete section of tiled wall from a tomb, the figures characteristically contorted so that the heads were in profile, the torso in front view, the limbs twisted without regard for anatomy. I knew it must have taken great effort—and some bending of the export law—to have obtained such a segment, and yet it reposed side by side with a plastic ikon. I went over to examine it. Mallory came up behind me, his shadow falling over the tiled surface like an adumbration of eternity.

"Well? What do you think of my atelier?"

"It's—crowded."

He laughed.

"My design," he said. "The modern and the ancient, side by side, as it should be."

"Even plastic?"

"Why not? Plastic has become the teak of our times."

Moving past the wall, I paused at a splendid mummy case that stood, upright and closed, in the corner. The surface was delicately carved, and the bright pigments had not faded badly. I spent a moment studying the case, then stepped to the side and discovered the modern world represented in its most definitive form—a chemist's bench. This explained why Arabella had referred to the workroom as a laboratory. The bench was lined with beakers of colored fluids, vials of exotic liquids, test tubes and a microscope, dried leaves and arcane herbs. I assumed Mallory must use these tools to determine chemically the age of his artifacts, and was about to interrogate him on his methods when I noticed what was perhaps the most remarkable object of all—remarkable in having no apparent function with regard to the other objects. It was a high flat platform with tubular steel legs and an arrangement of leather straps, not unlike an excruciatingly uncomfortable bed. Did Mallory, exhausted by his labors, crawl onto this curious table to sleep? I stared at the contraption, thinking it looked vaguely familiar, something about the leather straps— then I realized what it was. An operating table. What on earth was it doing here? I wondered. Had Snow examined Sam on this table? Or—I had a sudden image of Mallory performing some grisly dissection on his mummy, feverishly carving the withered flesh. The image was more unpleasant than the fact.

Mallory interrupted my macabre imaginings.

"But step over here," he said.

I followed him to a battered antique escritoire, incongruously equipped with a goose-necked lamp. A clay tablet rested on the surface, and observing the familiar hieroglyphs, I recognized it as the one I'd already translated from the photocopy. I examined it. Mallory sighed impatiently. After a moment he said, "You've already translated that, it's not important."

"I don't understand you. This is valuable."

"As an artifact? Can't I impress upon you that it is the content which is valuable, not the lump of clay?"

"You cannot. You've offered no reasons for such an astonishing assumption."

"Yes. Well, you will see. If this is what I think it is—" He conveyed a small silver casket to the front of the desk and then paused, idly caressing the elegantly chased lid. The casket still unopened, he peered at me thoughtfully. "You will continue to regard these translations as confidential, of course?"

"As you like," I retorted shortly, tired of such nonsense and wanting to get to work. Mallory nodded and opened the box, withdrew a papyrus scroll and unrolled the brittle yellow parchment. I spread it on the desk and bent over it, studying the markings.

Presently, I frowned.

"What's wrong?" he asked, looking worried.

"This isn't—properly—writing at all."

"What do you mean?"

"Not a form of written language. Some of it. See here—" I traced a forefinger across the parchment. "These pentagrams and symbols—and this, a diagram— This isn't something that can be translated as to connotation."

Mallory whitened, frowning.

"You can't do it?"

"Some of it. See—here are hieroglyphics. But the other symbols represent incantations as a whole. Not even verbal, perhaps."

"I don't understand."

"Look—can you see the difference between this papyrus and the writing on the tablet? The tablet is a block of hieroglyphic script, it can be translated word for word. But these symbols are the runic signs of the priests and magicians. It isn't a language. Possibly it doesn't even have meaning." Mallory was staring at me. "I can translate the hieroglyphs," I continued. "That's like any language. Certain signs represent particular sounds like the alphabet or certain objects, as in pictographic writing. But these diagrams can't be translated that way. They represent an idea, a concept, in total. There's no way to break down the significance piece by piece."

"I see," he muttered doubtfully.

"I might add that I've never seen anything quite like this scroll—the juxtaposition of symbol and pentagram, of common writing and mystic design. You may well have made an astounding discovery. But I'm afraid we have no Rosetta stone to reveal the meaning."

"You'll try?"

"Of course. But I cannot promise exactitude."

"Ashley, you have no idea how vital this is."

Mallory was tense and pale, his hands clenched.

"I'll do my best."

He nodded slowly and seemed about to say more, but his lips moved without sound. He nodded again. "I'll leave you alone then," he said. Mallory left the room. I sat down, bent the lamp to position, and commenced my work.

7

The papyrus was fine, made from Nile reed split into strips and pasted together with overlapping edges. A second sheet was placed at right angles to the first, for strength, and then pressed flat. The scroll consisted of several such sheets fastened end to end. The writing had been done with a pointed reed pen and ink fashioned of gum and carbon, and the script was in the cursive flowing hieratic common to the high priests. I had little difficulty with this hieratic writing itself, but the text was repeatedly interrupted by the insertion of the unknown diagrams and symbols. I struggled with these for some time, then abandoned them and began translating the remainder, hoping the meaning would become apparent through the translated text. It was slow work. I kept at it for several hours without pausing. Arabella came in at one point and left me a pot of coffee. I scarcely noticed her, although the coffee was welcome. Mallory also looked in several times from the door, but did not disturb my efforts.

Gradually a partial translation began to emerge, a line here and a line there, through persistence rather than inspiration. But there was no consistency. Each line was obscured by the interjection of one of the meaningless diagrams. I became frustrated: it almost seemed as though the long-dead scribe had deliberately obscured the meaning; as if he had written in code. I persevered, crumbling sheets of paper in annoyance, smoking my pipe aggressively, pausing to glare at ikons and figurines as if they were responsible for my difficulties. Presently I found my thoughts clouding with fatigue. I was making absurd mistakes. Perhaps Mallory's impatience had affected me, but haste is no virtue in work of this nature. I put down my pen and walked about the room while my head cleared, idly examining the remarkable profusion of artifacts and relics.

I came to the mummy case.

I wondered if the papyrus had come from this particular coffin; if it contained the mummy which Mallory claimed had been embalmed with its organs intact. Not wishing to open it without his permission, I contented myself with studying the carved inscriptions. They seemed familiar, and I looked closer. They were the same diagrams as those on the papyrus, the runic unknowns which I could not decipher. It shed no light on the problem, however. I passed my fingertips along the smooth wood, as if knowledge could seep into my mind through tactile contact, by some strange mental osmosis. My fingers seemed to tingle.

At the top of the case, where the head of the mummy should rest, was the typical winged disk supported on the outspread wings of a vulture. I had seen this common symbol many times, but it affected me now in a fanciful manner. What is as hideous as a scavenger, yet as necessary to nature's scheme? And how, too, like the mind of man—a creature which can soar above the clouds in glorious sunlight, and still must nourish its body in the filth of the earth. I thought of the

mummy within the case, of his life, of all the men of his time.
Were they so different from us? I wondered. Would I, granted
the impossible ability to journey to the Egypt of five thousand
years past, know the mood of the age as the ancients knew
it? And find it the same, perhaps? For like us, they had their
hopes, their dreams, their secrets.

It struck me like a bolt.

Secrets.

I stood very still, my mind turning over ponderously on the
shaft of insight.

I knew then what the papyrus was.

I rushed back to the desk and looked at it; in a moment I
saw that it was true, and stood open-mouthed, awed. The
document before me was the code book of the high priests,
the grimoire of the mystics. What I had taken for obscurity
was in fact clarity. In effect, I had been translating a translation. Some priest, daring the wrath of the gods, had on this
parchment set down the meanings of the sacred symbols
in the common language of his time. It was an electrifying
realization, an enormous find, comparable to the Rosetta
stone itself. All fatigue banished, I resumed my seat. Now it
was clear. The lines I had succeeded in translating defined the
diagrams which followed; the meanings were the same. The
papyrus gave the key to the arcane knowledge of the past,
the knowledge denied the common man and lost through
the ages. Almost afraid to touch such a document, I began to
work again.

Mallory came in some time later.

"Any progress?" he asked.

I turned in my chair and regarded him with a mixture of
effort and exaltation. My expression caused his eyes to glitter,
and he excitedly advanced across the room and stood over me
as I explained the true nature of the papyrus.

"Then you've found the key?"

"No, you found it—God knows how. I am simply turning it in the lock now."

"How long will it take?"

"How long? Does it matter? It's tremendously difficult, of course. Do you realize how hard it is to decode a message even in modern English? Well, imagine deciphering a code in a dead language. It will take some time."

"Time, yes. Always time," he muttered distastefully. I could not understand why it mattered. "I loath the concept of time," he grimaced, "the galling tyranny of an entity that endures forever while we must pass briefly through it. My great antagonist, time. And my great love. To master the secret of time—" He had gestured grandiloquently. Now he hesitated, looking somewhat sheepish. "You'll remain as long as necessary?"

"For this, yes."

He leaned over my shoulder, scrutinizing my scribblings, sensing my deep involvement.

"Can I help you in any way?" he asked.

I shook my head, wanting no more of his eccentric sophistries and obscure monologues. He continued to hang over me. "Of course," I said, "if you would explain exactly what you hope to find in these writings, it might help. I'd know, at least, what I was looking for."

"That would help?"

"Possibly."

He seemed to be debating with himself. I waited, gazing steadily at him. His shadow was cast away from the lamp and up the far wall, elongated, gaunt. I saw that it fell directly over the mummy case, as if it represented his spirit; as if his soul sought to enter the sarcophagus. Then he took a deep breath and drew a chair to the desk. He sat facing me, staring at me intently; so intently that I became uncomfortable.

"Well?"

He nodded once, slowly.

"Ashley, I am going to confide in you," he said.

I waited.

Lucian Mallory began his incredible tale.

Mallory started speaking slowly, as if ordering his thoughts and arranging them in a logical sequence. He said, "I believe I told you I'd found a mummy with both the internal organs and the brain intact?"

"You did."

"Did you believe me?"

"I don't know. The process of embalming was rooted in the myth of Osiris, you know. Set cut Osiris into pieces and scattered them in the desert, but Isis gathered the segments and put him together again, giving him immortality. Mummification was a literal reenactment of this legend. Any departure would seem to be at odds with their religion."

"I'm not talking of theology, but science."

"Weren't they the same?"

"Has it never occurred to you that there might have been more reason than a vague theology behind the process? More reason than adhering to an absurd myth?"

"Reason?" I said. "It was reason enough to the ancients. They could not conceive of a life other than physical, therefore they gained immortality in preserving the body. It's as much reason as most religions are based upon."

"Agreed, Ashley. But I told you, I am not speaking of religion. I mean true reasons, not belief. Fact, not faith. Suppose there were a physical reason to preserve the bodily tissue from decay?"

He seemed to expect an answer.

"Go on," I prompted.

"I'd often pondered that. Then, when I found my unusual mummy—that is true, by the way—it came to me. I perceived the meaning clearly." He paused to light a cigarette, the first I had ever seen him smoke. "You know, of course, that body tissue dies at different rates? That, for instance, the hair and fingernails may continue to grow—and therefore, to live—long after the other body cells are dead?"

I nodded. "Corpses have been disinterred and discovered to have long talons and hair, yes: it was formerly supposed they had been buried alive."

"Quite. Now consider this, Ashley. Suppose there were a process by which the brain cells continued to function after putative death?"

I thought. He watched me closely.

"After the body has died?" I said.

"Yes."

"Impossible."

He still was watching me, like a predator waiting to strike; some remarkable beast of prey which feasted upon the human imagination.

"Are you trying to tell me you believe this?"

"I know this."

"Let me get it straight. The body is actually dead. The heart no longer beats, the lungs no longer breathe, the blood no longer flows. All the symptoms of morbidity are present, the life processes are terminated. And yet the brain continues to live?"

"That is precisely what I mean."

"How long?"

He frowned and did not reply.

"Your instance of fingernails and hair—those cells live on for a certain duration, yes, but eventually they too die. It has been said that the head of a man, severed on the guillotine, lives for a few seconds as well. I might even concede that point. But are you speaking of a space of seconds, of minutes? Of hours?"

"I mean—indefinitely."

I stared at him.

"Forever, Ashley."

I continued to stare, wondering if this strange man possessed a sense of humor or if he were insane. But he seemed absolutely serious and convincingly sane. He also seemed concerned at my obvious disbelief. I still was uncertain whether I understood him. He had a habit of speaking in a circuitous manner, of obscuring his meanings, and perhaps I'd failed to grasp his point.

I said, "What do you mean by the brain?"

Mallory looked surprised.

"Why, the brain, no more and no less."

"Every function of the brain?"

"Yes."

"Awareness? Intelligence?"

"Yes, yes. The mind itself."

He tapped his head impatiently.

"But that is monstrous," I exclaimed. The full import of his statement struck me for the first time. It was impossible, of course, but even the theoretical concept was hideous. "You have a gruesome imagination, Mallory. A living, sentient brain, aware of its condition, encased within a decaying body? Knowing what was happening as its flesh rotted away and the maggots worked in its body? My God—"

"If the body decayed, yes. But if the flesh is preserved? What then, Ashley? Not preserved as the mummies we know, desiccated and withered, but capable of obeying the commands of the mind—able to move, to act, to live though dead —freed of the mortal shell. Is that monstrous, Ashley?"

"Yes," I shuddered, with chills ascending my backbone.

"No, no. Not monstrous. That is immortality."

He no longer appeared quite so sane. Or are such judgments in the eyes of the beholder, like beauty? Did the fevered glint in his gaze reflect from his unbalanced mind, or strike from within my perceptions?

"I can't believe you are serious," I said.

He scowled.

"Would Snow have come here, had I nothing to show him? No tangible results?"

"Snow? I thought he came to examine Sam?"

"Yes, yes. So he did. While he was here. But that was secondary, that was not the reason he came."

Neither of us spoke for some time. Mallory reached out to bend the lamp lower, and the shadows soared up the wall, becoming dimmer. He extinguished his cigarette. I noticed, with a singular clarity, that his fingernails were well cared for and that he wore a heavy gold ring on his third finger. The room was very quiet.

"Shall I continue?" he inquired at length.

I didn't want him to. I felt a revulsion toward both the man and his mad suppositions, but there was curiosity too, a morbid compulsion to listen to him; just as a passerby is attracted to the mangled remains of a sanguinary accident, so I was drawn to him, some gruesome gravity at work on my mind.

"Yes, continue," I said finally.

"Oh, there are difficulties, many difficulties, but I am on the threshold of success. Ashley, you doubt me now. Know this, then: for three weeks I kept a dog alive after the heart had stopped beating."

I shook my head. He ignored me.

"For ten days the dog was capable of motion. It walked, it wagged its tail, it scratched automatically at nonexistent fleas. There were no fleas. The dog's body was dead. After it could no longer walk it was still able to move its tongue, to open its eyes, to quiver with canine dreams. And even after all external signs of animation had ceased, it continued to register brain waves on my instruments. Ashley, it could have lived forever, had I known the process of preserving the flesh. That is what we must find in the ancient symbols." He was excited now, speaking frenetically and spraying saliva onto the desk. "With the dog, the blood began to congeal, the tissue to putrify. The brain continued to command the flesh, but soon the flesh had rotted and could not obey those commands. Do you under-stand? The brain can activate dead cells, but it cannot restore or replenish them. There is no digestive process, no way to assimilate fresh protein. As long as the original cells existed, they could function, but in that function they destroyed themselves. It is too soft, too weak, the living tissue. It must be preserved."

He suddenly snatched up the papyrus roll and shook it before me.

"Find me the secret of the flesh, Ashley!" he cried. "I have the secret of the mind! Between us we have the key to eter-nity!"

I stood up, alarmed by his abrupt movement.

Mallory bit his lip and put the papyrus down again. He seemed ashamed of his outburst, a man who did not wish to lose control of his behavior. His lips were wet with spittle. I did not like this, being closeted with a madman. And madness, it must be. Madness, it had to be. I did not wish to consider the alternative.

"Do you want to live forever, Mallory?" I asked, recalling that one should speak calmly to a lunatic.

He smiled.

"Of course," he said. "But even if I die—think of it—to die myself, and leave the legacy of immortality to mankind! To be the father of eternity! To be greater than Prometheus, bear-ing a gift far more magnificent than fire! If I die, Ashley, it will be as Osiris died—as a god!"

"You would use this process on man?"

"Why, what else? What other creature deserves it? Do you think it's not been done before? Perhaps the longevity of the Old Testament, certainly in Egypt, certainly in Haiti. I have invented nothing new but simply rediscovered the knowledge of the ancients. I have traced the course of this knowledge, seeing it fade in its journey, picking up a piece here, a piece there. I followed it up the Nile, pursued it through the African deserts and rain forests, traced the gulf where, in the galleys of foul slave ships, it crossed the Atlantic. I persevered, Ashley. At times I fell into despondency, feeling I should never gather up the thread, but I never doubted it existed. At times I was weak—like my mortal flesh, weak, weak. I flew into drunken rages and sank into sullen gloom. But always, in the end, like a lamp glowing in the distance, I was drawn once again on my quest. Perhaps it was predestined. Who knows? I know only what I have found, and what remains to be found." Mallory gestured, using both hands like a scale, weighing one against the other.

He spoke again.

"In Haiti," he said, "there are zombies."

I waited for a few seconds before commenting, "So I have heard, Mallory."

"You still doubt me, eh? Still, I can't blame you in your ignorance."

"Have you seen zombies?"

"No, I've not seen one. Not living. But I was able to gather the legends and to understand the realities. Zombies are not immortal, although they survive after death. They exist as the undead for seven years, so the legends go, and I have no cause to doubt that duration. Seven years, give or take a few months—better than I was able to do with the dog, Ashley. Far better." He shook his head morosely and then continued, "But only by duration. The zombies obey their masters and, in the end, are rewarded by peace. Just as the dog obeyed me. It looked at me with devotion in its dead eyes, even as they glazed. It licked my hand with its decaying tongue. Perhaps the dog knew what I had tried to give it. And, in the end, I rewarded it with peace. I destroyed its living brain. I am not a cruel man, Ashley. Once my experiment had failed." He sighed, and then his deep-set eyes once again glinted. "But you see, it need not fail in the future. Modern science gives us advantages that the Haitian witch doctors do not have. They have lost a great deal of the knowledge that was transported from Africa; carried in the minds of slaves, just as those slaves were carried in the stinking holds of ships. The art of preserving the flesh was partially lost. Or perhaps the necessary herbs and spices—chemicals, to us—were not available in the New World. Yet they retained enough skill to keep the brain alive for seven years, to anneal the flesh so that it did not corrupt; so that it endured until all the cells were exhausted by feeding upon themselves. But finally the tissue weakened and aged and could no longer function, although the brain lived on—although the mind survived within the brain."

"If that were true," I muttered, "these creatures went to their graves with awareness—they knew the fact; knew that they must lie immobile in their tombs through the ages." Mallory nodded quickly, excitedly, as if he thought I were beginning to believe him. But belief was not necessary. Even as an abstraction, the concept was sickening.

"But their masters were not always unkind," Mallory contended. "Even as I gave my faithful dog oblivion, so did they treat their servants—if the servant had been dutiful."

"How do you know that?" I asked.

Mallory leaned closer.

"I have seen, Ashley. With my own hands I have dug up the graves of the undead."

Such was the intensity of his expression, such the compulsion of his convictions, that I could not doubt him. I believed him deceived, mistaken, perhaps utterly insane, but did not for a moment doubt that he believed his own words. My revulsion now had ebbed. I was fascinated. I nodded for him to proceed.

"Three graves I found, Ashley, tracing them through squalid villages and sordid towns, asking questions of suspicious squint-eyed men and wretched plague-ridden women, of black sorcerers and wild hermits. They denied, they deceived, they fled, but I never doubted; I pleaded, I bribed, I threatened, and, in the end, I found what I sought. Three graves, Ashley, in the mountain fastness where few white men have ever ventured. They were unmarked, grown over, secreted. I rooted them out like a voracious swine greedily snuffling after truffles. The first two graves were the same. The corpse had decayed, brittle bones lay in peaceful death, the skulls were picked clean and empty. But, Ashley—in both those graves I found that a wooden stake had been driven through the eye sockets. The stakes remained, upright in the skulls, and the skulls were void of contents."

A faint smile flitted fleetingly over his cavernous countenance. "Do you understand what this meant, Ashley? Those men had been fortunate. They had merciful masters to destroy the brain before consigning their servants to the grave. I saw it instantly. These men had served well and were deserving of peace. By destroying the continuity of the brain itself, the mind was released, the brain could die. The stake had deprived it of the ability to function, to survive; no longer must it preserve its own matter from decay. By these negative discoveries, I strengthened my own convictions. It was logical. It was fundamental. It could be traced back even to the legend of the vampire, the wooden stake through his heart to bring him peace, although the myth had mutated; it was not the heart that must be spitted upon the stake, but the brain. I was overjoyed. I saw that the lost knowledge was even more widespread than I'd hoped, directly linked to the vampires of the Balkans, the jaguar men of South America, the crocodile men of the tropical rain forests of equatorial Africa; that it was more ancient than the pyramids; that some primeval ancestor of man, mixing herbs and roots with evolutionary curiosity, might well have created the immortal gods before mortal man existed. Ashley, I knew then I was on the right track, I knew I was destined to find this lost knowledge. Ashley, I have—"

He paused.

I was captivated beyond skepticism.

"And the third grave, Mallory?" I asked.

"The third grave," he repeated.

He looked directly into my eyes.

"In the third grave I found proof.

"High in the central mountains, deep in brooding mahogany forests where stunted thorn trees claw at barren cliffs and the wind beats at the land with a pulsing rhythm compelling as the voodoo drums, I found the third grave. A mound of earth, no more, unmarked, unhallowed. I stood over it for a long while, certain at last that I'd found my proof. The trees were grotesquely malformed by the wind and twisted away on all sides as though I stood in the vortex of a storm—as though the trees themselves, living creatures, were cringing back from that unholy grave. I stood in awe, in dread, horrified at what I hoped to find. And then, at last, I opened the earth. I had a spade, the grave was shallow, within minutes I uncovered bone. There was no coffin, the corpse had been placed naked in the ground. I cast the spade aside and cleared the dirt away with my bare hands, gently, carefully, without disrupting the skeleton. The task done, I stood back and surveyed from a distance, delaying for final delicious and terrible moments my ultimate examination. The bones lay at a contorted posture, as if frozen forever at an instant of writhing agony. Only a few dried shards of flesh remained on the rib cage, the thigh. The burial garment had rotted to foul shreds. I regarded the skull. It was tilted at the neck. The empty eye sockets were black, the teeth thrust upward in a fleshless grimace.

"I knelt beside the skeleton.

"I straddled it, on hands and knees.

"I lowered my face over the skull, as if to breathe life into drowned lungs.

"I looked into the empty eye sockets.

"And there, Ashley, there within the naked bone, the living brain remained—"

I recoiled from his words as from a blow, then leaned back toward him as though drawn by perverse fascination. I mumbled something, God knows what, and he nodded.

"Yes, the brain lived," he said.

"My God."

"The worms do not devour living tissue, Ashley—they had spurned the brain while gorging on the body. I crouched over the skeleton feeling—what did I feel? I'd found the proof I needed, but the horror—I am not immune to horror. I felt a bond of brotherhood with that abomination; we were stamped from the same mold, pressed from the same template, shared the same human sentience. I spoke to the creature, my warm breath fell over it. It was not aware of me, of course. Its senses had withered with its flesh, it could not see or hear or feel. But Ashley, there is no doubt—it could think!"

I tried to speak. My vocal cords rebelled.

"And what did it think, Ashley, through the long decaying years? What does the mind think when it is divorced from all bodily sensations? Does it lose awareness, or gain? Does it sink into darkness, forgetting, becoming clouded without external stimuli? Or does it perhaps expand, grow, become a thing of higher evolution once it has been freed from the carnal dungeon? I did not know then, I do not know now. I was faced with terrible alternatives. I strained in silence, thinking to hear the creature's brain waves within my own mind; thinking, devoid of physical bondage, it might have developed senses beyond human limitations. But I felt no transmission. I had to decide. I am not unmerciful, the fear of destroying something finer than mortal man wrenched my mind asunder. Yet I could not know, there could be no certainty. I wished for an encephalograph to read the patterns of those impulses; perhaps to devise a code by which I could understand them, could communicate with its mind. But there in the high forest I had no equipment, I had only my erring human judgment."

He shook his head sadly, regretfully.

"I could not remove the body. There already had been some difficulty over the opening of graves; I was hounded by blind authority. No, there were but two choices, and both were immediate. Night was coming on with tropical suddenness, the wind fashioned a threnody in the mahogany trees. At last, in agony, I made my decision.

"I cut a sharp stake from a satinwood limb.

"I had no mallet, I chose a heavy rock. The scene is engraved upon my memory. I remember it all in every detail. There was green moss on the rock, living moss; a small mammal scurried through the undergrowth; the shadows were long and jagged but for two; these, cast by storm-ravaged trees, intersected at the grave, adumbrating a cruciform symbol. I am no Christian, Ashley, and yet this shadowed cross struck a primitive chord in my senses. Perhaps it was this that caused my decision, who knows? I knelt once more beside the skeleton. I took the stake in my left hand and placed the sharpened point into the eye socket. With my right hand I raised the stone. My hand trembled. A bit of moss fell from the rock and fluttered onto the skull.

"I spoke to the skull.

"'Forgive me, if I am wrong,' I said.

"And I drove the stake into the brain—"

"It was gruesome. The brain is more resilient than one imagines, and the stake recoiled. I struck again and then again. Slowly the wood was driven down into the viscous mass, each blow dull, muted. In a frenzy I slammed the rock down time and again. One blow missed, crushing the front of the skull. Brain matter extruded from the eye sockets. It sickened me. I closed my eyes and struck once more, and it was finished.

"I had given him peace?

"Or had I committed murder?"

He stared at me, expecting an answer, convinced—through his own conviction—that I believed his tale. And I? Did I believe him, then? Had we been in the Red Lion, my own cottage, on neutral ground, I'd have thought it the babbling of a madman. But there, surrounded by his relics in that stone-walled chamber—it was a setting conducive to belief. Doubt was enfeebled by circumstance. The rational surface of my mind proclaimed it impossible, but from beneath that calm surface erupted bubbles of emotion, dragons from the depths of the id. And as they rose, the rational surface rippled.

"How can it be?" I asked him—and myself, as well—shaking my head. The motion served only to jostle my thoughts about within my mind. "The brain cannot exist without the body. It demands the body, it requires glandular secretions, nutrients, oxygen, blood—the brain is not the soul, Mallory, it cannot rise from the corpse." He was frowning at me. "Why, one-fourth of all the blood pumped from the heart goes to service the brain."

"Yes. A huge percentage, considering the relatively small mass. That disproves nothing. On the contrary, it attests to the overwhelming power of the brain—the subservience of the body. And the mind—is that not the soul?—what does the mind need with a pump to push its blood when it can suck up the very substance of thought? What does it want with the cumbersome process of digestion, excretion, circulation? They are useless appendages to man, vestigial traits from the dawn of time when we came crawling and dripping from the primordial slime. The brain is a tyrant ruling imbecilic cells and yet unable to renounce its corporal kingdom. Yet it lives royally. Do you know that the human brain receives the same amount of blood every moment through its existence? That cerebral vessels are not affected by heat or cold or physical exertion but take their due unaltered, no matter how the muscles labor? Are you not convinced?"

I did not wish to be convinced.

If this were truth, I would deny truth. I turned away from him, I stared sightless about the room, all perceptions turned inward, my thoughts horrendous. I pictured a man, any man, myself perhaps, the body dead and the mind aware, waiting, waiting—patiently waiting for corruption. The thoughts, my God, the thoughts, untempered by sensation, that would exist without that mind! Would he pray the maggots speed, would he will them first to his eyes so that, blinded, he need not witness his own decay? Would he silently scream for the skulking scavenger whose dripping jaws could crush the skull? I wanted to vomit. It could not be. Mallory had sought proof, and now I sought proof to disprove. My eyes, wandering, suddenly focused.

I was looking at the mummy case.

Mallory intercepted my gaze.

"Yes," he nodded. "I will show you my mummy."

I followed Mallory across the room, holding tight rein on my emotions, telling myself this was merely another mummy like many another I had seen. Mallory put his hand on the edge of the case, then paused dramatically, like a magician about to produce a rabbit from a hat. He was facing me; peering at me, not at the case. Then he threw it open.

The mummy moved.

I screamed silently within my head and leaped back.

Mallory, still watching me, chuckled.

My inflamed imagination was roaring like a forest fire, and I had to struggle with myself to keep from bolting. The mummy had made a solitary motion; now it was still. I saw that it had been placed so that the arms, folded over the chest, had been held in position by the lid of the case; that, when Mallory threw the lid back suddenly, the arms had dropped down to the sides. One clawlike hand came to rest on the edge of the case. It had been—or so it seemed in my fevered state —a remarkably lifelike motion. Thank God my scream had been silent, I thought, seeing Mallory's amusement. My startled leap had been embarrassing enough.

Looking as nonchalant as I could, I stepped forward.

"A pretty fellow, eh?" Mallory said.

I grimaced.

"I call him Encephalon."

I inspected the mummy. Someone—Mallory, presumably —had unwound the wrappings from head and torso, leaving only the flanks and lower limbs bound in yellowed linen. The mummy was blackened and withered and loathsome. The mottled skin was drawn tautly over a gaunt rib cage and sunken belly, and crouching upright on spindly thighs it seemed possessed of a terrible vitality; the mummy seemed frozen at an instant of energy.

I looked at the face.

The features were perfectly preserved, although age had blotched the skin. Two dull grey eyes, without pupils, congealed like drops of lead in the eye sockets. The thin lips had shriveled back from irregular yellow fangs.

Mallory was watching me with interest.

"Hideous," I said.

Mallory carefully tucked the errant claw back inside the case. My initial impression satisfied, I regarded the mummy with more professional interest. The torso had been neatly slit below the breastbone but not in the manner of the ancient embalmers. The cut looked surgical and recent.

"You've opened it?" I asked.

"Of course. This is my cut." He pointed to the belly. "You will notice there are no others—the corpse was embalmed without being gutted."

"Unusual."

"Yes. But see here—and here—" He was thrusting his forefinger from place to place on chest and flank. His finger touched the marcescent skin. I saw the slight indentations where he pointed and leaned closer. They appeared to be puncture wounds which had drawn closed as the flesh tightened. "It was through these openings that the chemicals were passed into the body cavity—poured, injected, dripped, however it was done." He shrugged. "I know nothing of their methods, other than that they succeeded—but succeed, they did, for look—"

Mallory tenderly spread open the incision below the breast-bone, stretching the parchment-like flesh. I looked. There within the dark body cavity, hardened and dried but positioned as in life, were the mummy's internal organs.

"Remarkable," I said, almost forgetting Mallory's previous revelations as my interest was arrested by this astonishing discovery. But it was not a simple variation in the embalming process that he was showing me, and letting the belly close up again, he reached to the bony head.

He cupped the cheeks in both hands and turned the head to the side.

"See them?"

I saw. At the temple and below the ear and at the base of the skull were further punctures.

"The same process?"

"Yes. The same method, although the fluids employed were different. More effective, apparently."

"How so?"

He smiled meaningfully.

He turned the head to the other direction.

I gasped.

Mallory had opened an oblong hole in the skull, removing a segment of bone and exposing the brainpan. And in that hollow was the brain. I stared at it, my mouth gaping open. The brain was not hardened and dried like the organs—it was soft and pulpy, it seemed almost to pulsate with life. This was no embalming process known to man—no process I had ever conceived of. Whatever methods had been used, this brain was preserved as it had been in life.

I turned to stare at Mallory.

"And now," he said. "Now do you believe?"

"I don't know what to believe."

"Come now. Skepticism is all well and good, but you can't deny what you've seen. Or do you suppose I'm playing a hoax? That I've stuffed this skull with some plastic simulation?"

"No, not that."

"Well then?"

"It's—it's inconceivable. But—it's there, I can't deny that. As to the other—do you really believe that brain still lives?"

Mallory frowned slightly and, before he replied, turned the head back to the front.

"That, I don't know," he said. "Nothing registers on the encephalograph. Too long entombed, perhaps? Or faultily prepared? What is life? We cannot define it. This is living matter, no doubt. But as to whether it can still think—that is the question again, Ashley. Perhaps through the ages the brain, without external stimuli, sinks into a state of mental inertia. Several times I've been tempted to take pity on him —to destroy his brain. But it is too precious. He's lived inside that skull for five thousand years; a few more years wouldn't hurt him, if a sense of duration still exists. Or, without the senses, can the passage of time exist at all?" Mallory peered at me bemusedly. "Ah, Ashley, there are so many things I do not yet understand. But I know the most important, I know how this brain was preserved. I took a small section of tissue—not enough to damage it—and the chemical analysis was simple enough. It was by duplicating that process that I kept—kept the dog alive."

"And the organs?"

"That is where I have failed. You saw how hardened they were. Analysis proves nothing. That is why I'm so desperately hoping you'll be able to discover the process in your translations."

"But—if it didn't work for this man—"

"That means nothing. Men die on the operating table every day. It could have been a mistake, a blunder, the wrong combination of chemicals. Or perhaps it did not fail. Perhaps Encephalon lived for a thousand years, two thousand—perhaps there was some scale by which the ancients judged a man's worth and granted him a specific duration of life after death. Perhaps they did not have true immortality with their primitive chemistry—but today, with all the benefits of science, if once we make a beginning we shall surely be able to extend the span into eternity."

"Does the end justify the means?"

"Certainly," said Mallory.

He proceeded to close the mummy case, then paused and patted the mummy fraternally on the shoulder before drawing shut the lid. He turned to me, smiling, as though I were presumed an accomplice and collaborator. And was I? Did I see him as he saw himself, the would-be benefactor of mankind? Or as some dark angel with flaming sword, barring man from whatever paradisiacal domain Heaven affords?

"I'll leave you to your work now," he said.

He started for the door.

"Mallory!"

He turned back.

"All this that you've told me—"

"Yes?"

"Did you—tell Amos Snow?"

He regarded me thoughtfully.

Then he shrugged.

"What does it matter?" he said. "The man is dead."

He left. The door closed very solidly behind him. The room was silent. I stood there, alone. No, not alone. I stood there with Encephalon.

8

I do not pretend to remember the sequence of my thoughts, for my mind dashed madly from point to point, as if describing the geometries of deduction. I sat at the desk, the papyrus before me, but I could not concentrate on it. My eyes kept edging toward the mummy case, toward my eerie companion. I hadn't the slightest doubt Mallory had killed Snow; that he had revealed his knowledge to Snow, and the doctor had refused to cooperate, perhaps had threatened to expose him and his intentions. Just as he'd revealed it to me—the similarities were too obvious. We had both been summoned here for our specific abilities—had both been told the reasons—had rejected Mallory's design.

I was afraid.

I did not fear Mallory; my fear arose from a deeper source, welling up from basic instincts too primitive to countenance the rational mind.

I did not admit it to myself.

Not at first.

It was nonsense.

Yet my eyes returned to the mummy case.

No, I told myself. Mallory killed Snow, not—

Not something else.

But Snow's body had been horribly mangled, almost dismembered by inhuman force. Mallory did not look powerful, he was tall and gaunt. Mallory did not seem the type to fly into an uncontrollable rage, even if he possessed the strength. Mallory was not the sort to commit his own crimes, but to summon another to the task.

Once again my eyes turned to the mummy case.

I could no longer deny my thoughts.

To summon another—

It was not possible—

Or was it?

Could that gruesome thing live?

Had that long-dead corpse been used to commit murder?

I shuddered, my flesh crept over my bones. "I call him Encephalon," Mallory had said. Had he spoken in the literal sense? Did he mean that he truly called it? Called it up from the dead ages, from the tomb? An image burned itself into my mind. I saw Mallory standing before the opened sarcophagus, heard his voice intone the words, saw the withered creature begin to stir, the leaden eyes commence to glow, the first unsteady footfall as it stepped from the mummy case—as it stepped out from death itself.

No!

I would not allow myself such madness.

I rose from the desk and walked steadily across the room. I didn't hesitate. I flung open the case. Encephalon crouched within, blackened, dead. I almost laughed at my imagination, at the courage it had taken to open that case, at the absurdity of my fancy. I started to close it again, then paused.

The room was silent.

It always happened in silence.

The silence of the pyramid, the silence of the arch—

Faintly, faintly, deep inside my head, I heard a sound. It was a ripple, a rustle, a trickle, something so basic that I could not comprehend it. It grew no stronger. It wavered. It was beyond hope, beyond sorrow. Then I knew. I knew that the human mind, in solitude through millenniums, would not evolve. It would devolve. It would not register waves that were discernible to our instruments, any more than we could read the thought patterns of the amoeba. We had been creatures without thumbs, without vocal cords, without spines; such we could be once more.

Such was Encephalon.

I closed the case.

I no longer feared the mummy, for I'd known its weakness, known the helplessness within that withered skull. I no longer feared death itself, for there are far worse things than death. I stood there in the silence, and my living flesh crawled with maggots of horror.

I could work no more.

I could bring myself to remain in that chamber no longer. I arranged the papers and the scroll on the desk and, with a final glance at the mummy case, left the workroom. Retracing my steps down the dark corridor, I came to the door of Sam's cell. It was still barred. Something sparked in my mind, it seemed I should remember something, make some deduction, draw some conclusion, but my thoughts were erratic with the terrible knowledge I had engulfed; concentration was beyond me. Later there would be time to think, I told myself, and I continued on. The corridor opened into the main hallway. There I encountered Mallory.

"Have you any results?" he asked.

"Nothing further."

"Ah. What did you want?"

"I'm exhausted, Mallory. I'll have to rest for a while."

He looked perturbed.

"I suppose so," he conceded grudgingly.

"If I continue now, I'll make mistakes."

"No, we can't allow mistakes," he agreed. "Forgive me. You can understand my impatience."

I nodded.

"Will you eat now?"

"I think not."

"Shall I have Arabella bring food to your room?"

I started to protest that I had no appetite, then paused. It occurred to me that there were questions I could well put to Arabella. I nodded.

"You'll return to work soon?"

"Soon, Mallory."

Satisfied, he moved down the somber paneled hall. I watched him. I saw how thin he was, how narrow his shoulders. No, he could no more have torn Amos Snow apart than could that bloodless mummy—that mummy at the end of the dark corridor—the corridor with the barred door—the door behind which Sam Cooper was locked. Sam Cooper was a strong man, big, broad. My shoulder twitched with physical recall as I remembered how easily he had struck John aside; how he had lifted me effortlessly from the cobblestones.

Lifted me toward his face—

His mouth—

Inspector Peal's words rushed at me.

"The flesh torn—by human teeth—"

I went to my room.

I was stretched out on the bed when Arabella knocked at the door. I'd been thinking. There was much to consider. I jumped up and called for her to enter, and she did so, carrying a tray. She put it down and began to arrange dishes and utensils. Suddenly she laughed, perhaps regarding herself ill-suited to this menial task and, still laughing, said, "I'm the cook, too."

"I'm sure you're a good one."

"I'm terrible. Lucian doesn't seem much interested in food."

"What about Sam?"

She looked at me.

"Does Sam have a good appetite? I suppose you have to prepare his meals, too?"

"That's a curious thing," she murmured. "Lucian always attends to that himself. He told me Dr. Snow had made certain dietary suggestions. But it's strange. I've never seen Lucian preparing his meals, and I've never noticed any food gone from the larder." She shrugged. "Well, maybe he has some special stuff—like fat women, you know. Or perhaps you don't know. All the calories and nutrients in a formula. Or maybe I've just not noticed. After all, he has to eat something, doesn't he?"

"Did Mallory tell you—before you came here—that you'd be caring for an imbecile?"

"Sam?"

"Yes."

"Oh, Sam wasn't deranged when I first came, you know. He was perfectly normal. A very pleasant man."

"What?"

"Why, what did you think? No, Sam's accident happened only last week."

"He fell down stairs?"

"Yes."

"You—didn't see the accident?"

"No. I saw him just afterward."

"I was under the impression," I countered, "that it happened some time ago."

"You must have misunderstood."

"You're certain?"

"Of course." She looked as though my question were foolish, which I suppose it was. She said, "It was fortunate that Dr. Snow was visiting here when it happened. Lucian says Sam would have died, if he hadn't had expert medical attention immediately."

Things clamped together in my mind, gears meshed and turned other pieces.

"Do you know why Snow was here?"

"Why, not really. He was interested in Lucian's theories, I suppose. I know they spent lots of time in the workroom. But I'm not sure just why. I mean—a brain surgeon and an Egyptologist seemed an unlikely coupling."

"Doesn't it, though."

"Is something wrong, Thomas?"

"I'm afraid something is dreadfully wrong."

She regarded me levelly, still holding a fork in her hand, staring across the table.

"What is it?"

"Arabella, did you see Snow examine Sam?"

"No. But that's only natural. I mean, he wouldn't want me looking over his shoulder. But I was off somewhere when Sam fell. Let's see. Yes, I was in the garden. Lucian thought he'd left his cigarette case there and sent me to fetch it. Turned out he'd merely left it in another jacket. I came back just as the three of them were going to the laboratory—the workroom, I mean. I could tell right away that something was wrong, because Snow and Lucian both looked, well, worried, I guess. That is, I didn't think they looked worried at the time, Snow looked more sort of frightened, but afterward I saw they must have been worried because Sam was injured."

My voice interrupted tersely, "And Sam? Was he unconscious?"

"No, he was walking. I thought later that was strange, but at the time, of course, I didn't know he'd been hurt. But it was a curious thing. Sam seemed perfectly normal before Snow examined him. He turned and winked at me. I think he fancied me, poor man. Then Lucian told me to go to my room, that they had important work. Later he came to my room and told me how Sam had fallen down the stairs and injured his head and how Snow had managed to save his life but feared he was permanently affected. It was a complete surprise to me, especially after Sam had appeared so normal the last I saw him. I asked Lucian about it, as a matter of fact. He said that head injuries often took a course like that. Delayed effect, or something, he said. Even then, I wasn't prepared for it when I saw Sam again. I felt so badly about it. And he's getting worse, you know." She paused and assumed a pained expression before continuing quietly, "I suppose he'll die. At first he was just, well, dazed, but in the last few days he's been so violent.

He gets the most terrible look in his eyes. And Lucian has taken to locking him in his room."

"When did he start—locking him in?"

"Just yesterday. After he returned from town. I suppose because of what happened with father."

I was gnawing my lip.

"I'm sure that Lucian doesn't take proper care of him, Thomas. I can't understand why he insists on keeping him here. And Sam, poor Sam—he can't even bathe himself, I suppose. I know he's starting to smell bad."

"Oh, my God."

My words frightened her.

"What is it, Thomas?"

I shook my head.

"Please, what's wrong?"

I stared at her. Why was she here? I said, "His talk of—immortality. Has he promised you that?"

"Well, he did, actually," she confessed with an embarrassed smile. "He's always talking about how we would live forever. He's such a strange man, he sounded as if I was supposed to take him seriously. It's hard to tell when he jokes that way. But of course he must have been joking. Or else I didn't understand him."

"Arabella, he was perfectly serious."

"Serious? But how could he be. I mean, he's not crazy."

"No, he's not crazy. But what could be more serious than immortality? Something worse than madness drives him toward—toward something yet worse. Arabella? Would you want to live forever?"

She smiled bemusedly and perceived that I too was speaking in a serious manner of impossible things. "I don't know. I've never considered it, really. I guess I'm a practical girl at heart. But please, Thomas. Tell me what is wrong?"

"I can't. Not yet."

"Are you—planning to do something?"

I nodded grimly. I was indeed planning to do something, and it was not something I anticipated with pleasure. Already my spine was tingling.

"I have to see Sam," I said.

"I'm sure Lucian—"

"Without Lucian. Definitely without Lucian."

"He's been so frenzied, Thomas. Should you go to his room alone?"

Perhaps not.

Perhaps I should go, instead, out the battered oaken door and down the weed-engulfed drive and along the hedgerow-rimmed road until I came to Farriers Bar. Perhaps then I should speak to Inspector Peal, who would not believe me, and board the first train back to London where I quite remorselessly might suppress all conscious recollection of Lucian Mallory and Sam Cooper and Encephalon and Egypt and all things proper for mortal man to forget. Perhaps I should live at my cottage in blissful oblivion and grow old through a normal span.

But I would not do that. I could not walk away from this without knowing. Perhaps I could not even walk away at all, for Amos Snow had departed this house, knowing precisely what I knew, and Amos Snow's cadaver had been found by Melville Coots, mangled and torn. I did not want my body found, not that way, not yet, although I was very certain that someday I intended to die. That gave me courage. Perhaps it was the courage of desperation, but it was not false. Every man, born, owes a debt to death, and that debt must be paid. One day it must be paid. I felt rather calm and determined. Arabella was still standing there across the table, staring at me, not understanding whatever expression had come over my countenance. Nor did I care to explain. I left her there, went down the stairs, and without hesitating once I proceeded directly to that barred door in the dark corridor. I did hesitate then, but only for a moment.

Then I lifted the bar.

Sam was on the bed.

I stood at the open door, allowing my eyes to adjust to the gloom. The chamber was small and cold, illumined by misty grey light venturing ineffectually through a high leaded window. The window was unlatched, accounting for the chill, but nevertheless the air seemed heavy with an offensive odor. Sam did not move. I thought he was sleeping and moved closer, then saw that his eyes were wide open, staring sightlessly at the ceiling. They looked strange, dull, like the eyes of Encephalon; as if no moisture remained in them. I stood beside the bed. He continued to ignore me. "Sam?" I said. There was no response. I bent down. The stench arose to assail my senses. I reached out, and my hand hesitated willfully, hovering in the air, trembling with reluctance. My hand was only mortal, it rebelled. I had to force it down, onto his breast. He made no move as I touched him. He didn't move at all. Nothing moved on that bed. Sweat was running down my face and neck, despite the cold, but Sam's face was dry. Even his mouth was dry; he no longer drooled uncontrollably, and his lips seemed to have darkened and shriveled back from his teeth.

His hand was at his side.

I touched the wrist with my fingertips.

The flesh was cold and nothing moved. I felt that cold run up my fingers, along my arm, down my spine.

I stood back, looking at him with horror.

Suddenly Sam's head wrenched toward me.

Yellow eyes writhing, he glared at me.

His face started to change. It changed as no human face ever should. I was at the door before I was aware of moving; through the entrance and hurling the door closed behind me. I saw movement at the last moment, through the angle, and then the door slammed shut. I dropped the heavy bar into place. Just as the bar struck, solidly, the massive door shuddered and exploded from within. It jarred within the frame, just once, and the sound echoed in the passage. Then it was still. It's all right now, I told myself. But it was not all right. Nothing was all right. I raised my hand and stared at my fingers. They seemed alien, transformed by tactile contact, cold, bloodless.

Sobbing, I walked back down the corridor.

The foul stench was still in my nostrils.

I knew what it was.

I had touched him; I knew.

No heart beat within his breast, no blood pulsed in his wrist, the stench was that of decaying flesh. I had not entered a room; I had entered a grave.

Mallory was in his study, a rather barren room with unadorned walls and a window overlooking the crumbling outbuildings and stone fences. He was smoking. I entered without a word, and he peered at me expectantly: "Returning to work now?" Then he saw my expression and frowned.

"I've just come from Sam's room."

"Oh? That was rather—daring."

"I know, Mallory. I know what Sam is. God knows how or why, but I touched him. Mallory, what fiendish thing have you done?"

Mallory sighed.

"Well, there's no help for it," he said. "I suppose you had to know eventually. But you're an intelligent man, Ashley. You must understand."

"Was Snow not intelligent?"

He gave me a sharp look. He hesitated, perhaps debating whether to essay deceit, then shrugged once more. "Snow was a doctor," he said. "They have those damnable ethics. Yes, he was intelligent, but he was a captive within his own code of behavior."

"Like Sam is a captive in that room?"

"Eh? Ah, well, captivity takes many forms. Sam's body is imprisoned in a cold room, but, more to the point, Sam's mind is hopelessly entrapped within his cold body. That is regrettable. As I've told you, I am never deliberately cruel. I didn't wish to hurt Snow, you understand. I trusted him. As I've trusted you, Ashley. But he betrayed me, he refused to help me. I had to force him. Then, after it was done, he escaped. I wasn't careful enough, I was too excited about the experiment." He stubbed his cigarette out and immediately lighted another. "Still, perhaps it was better. Otherwise I'd have had to keep him indefinitely, at great trouble."

"He—operated on Sam?"

"He infused the chemicals, yes."

"And—" Even knowing what I did, it was difficult to utter the words: "And killed him?"

"In a manner of speaking. Death—bodily death—appears to be a necessary side effect of the process. It was the same with the dog. Perhaps the chemicals themselves cause it, or perhaps the brain, preserved, simply wills termination of the other physical functions. I can't really say, as yet. I'd hoped Snow would be able to tell me."

"But why, Mallory? Why did you do it?"

"Why?" He seemed surprised.

"Why destroy Sam?"

"Ashley, Ashley, don't you understand? Sam is far more than he was."

"More? My God, man. He's rotting!"

"Yes, I'm afraid he is. But he isn't the first. Many men, better men than Sam, have lain living in their graves as the long years toll and have persisted within the silence of their skulls. Is one more so important?"

"Mallory—I'll grant you're seeking something—something you consider good. But you've admitted yourself that you haven't discovered the process of preserving the flesh. You deliberately condemned Sam to living corruption."

"Regrettably, yes. But I had to be sure, Ashley. I am no surgeon. When I treated the dog's brain, and the animal died, how could I know but what my own clumsy efforts were responsible? The process took effect, yes, but how could I tell what was part of the process and what was caused by my own blunders. The brain is a complex thing, Ashley. It can't be chiseled like a block of granite. I'd hoped that under Snow's skilled hands, Sam would truly live."

He spoke as if it were a calculated risk; as if it were perfectly reasonable.

"And Sam's madness? The loss of mental facilities?"

Mallory grimaced.

"Another blunder," he conceded, turning up his palms. "Snow was too nervous. I expect that's understandable, given the circumstances. His scalpel slipped, cut a few millimeters too deeply or on the wrong tangent. Perhaps, who knows, it was deliberate. What he might have considered a mercy killing. But make no mistakes, Ashley. The process was absolutely successful. The infusion into the brain matter worked just as I had predicted. The insanity—well, that was merely a side effect, a fractional error of trembling fingers. The next time, he would have avoided that."

I was stunned. "The next time?"

"Of course."

"Who, Mallory?"

He looked away.

"Arabella?"

"Well—perhaps. Only if I was certain of success, you understand. Arabella, young and beautiful forever—" I was controlling myself with great difficulty. He did not seem aware of this, enveloped in a frenzy of oneiric imaginings. He said, "But Sam can still be saved. It isn't too late. It's up to you now."

"Me? I want no part of this."

Mallory cocked his head.

"But, Ashley. If you can decipher the ancient knowledge, if you can discover the related process of preserving the body, Sam will live. Insane, yes, but alive. That should appeal to your ethics, does it not? And think, Ashley! If you fail, think what Sam must endure."

I could only stare at him.

"Perhaps, in a fashion, it's just as well that Sam is deranged," he said, trying to placate me. "Grief, horror, all the emotions, are caused only by chemical imbalance in the brain. Sam can feel no emotions now. Except the most basic—" He paused thoughtfully. I walked over to the window and gazed out. It was darkening now, and the stone fences emerged like some obscure maze set to confound the minds of men. But they had crumbled in many places, and would not have the span of the pyramids. I could feel Mallory's eyes at my back. When I turned he continued to stare at me, judging, deliberating.

"How can you know what Sam feels?" I asked.

"A good point," he said. "I thought I knew, but after—after the lad was killed—"

I'd forgotten young Brooke; that bucolic tragedy seemed to have no place in this terrible scheme. I moved back to his desk.

"Sam killed them both?"

Mallory nodded.

"For God's sake, why? Why the boy?"

"There have been so many mistakes, Ashley. I suppose it must ever be so as we stumble blindly after new secrets. I'd had to send Sam after Snow, you understand that. He escaped, and I couldn't allow him to destroy all that I've strived for. I sent Sam after him. Sam can move quickly once his course is determined. It takes a considerable time for his initial movements, but after the impulse is finally sent out he commands great speed and unbelievable strength. He went out with the bandages still swathed around his head, the loose ends trailing down his back. I wasn't sure he would succeed. You may well imagine with what anxiety I awaited his return. He was gone for some time. Then he came back. His hands and face were bloody, and I knew then that it was all right. Well, not all right but—necessary."

Drained of emotion, I asked, "And the boy?"

"Ah. You gave me quite a shock when you told me about that. It was Sam, of course. I'd taken no precautions; I had no reason to think him dangerous. Why did he kill a second time?" He gestured, palms rotating. "I've a couple theories about that. Who knows how a deranged mind works, even in a living body? Some shred of memory retention remaining, perhaps? Once instructed to kill, he remembered the command? Took it as a constant? I think that likely. Or can it be that he is now reduced to the basic drive of carnivore man? He no longer has a sex drive, he requires no food, no warmth. Is bloodlust more basic than any impulse? It may well be, Ashley. Sad but true. Our ancestors had no sex drive, they reproduced by splitting themselves apart. Plants need food, they produce their own. But the need to destroy other organic matter—is that not the root of all living behavior, the common denominator, the initial impulse sparking the first life at the dawn of time?" Mallory sneered and directed a plume of smoke toward the ceiling. "A question for the philosophers, that. I can't pretend to know. It might be far more simple, perhaps an effect of the chemicals Snow infused in his brain. As his own blood dries up, does he feel the urge for that of others?" He expelled a long breath. "Well, in time we will know these things. But, for the moment, I only know he has the urge to kill."

"And his great strength?"

"Interesting, that. But quite simple. He has the strength of the madman. He is bound by no inhibitions, he can feel no pain, he has the power of total concentration on his purpose. He is almost invulnerable, Ashley. His nervous system, his arteries, pain centers, bones—they are dead. He could exert himself on an impossible task until his very skeleton snapped apart. He cannot be wounded. Great holes might be torn in his flesh, he would feel nothing; he would not even bleed much, for blood does not flow when the heart no longer pumps." Mallory was totally engrossed in his thoughts as he continued, "It will be enlightening—if you fail, Ashley—to see how he deals with a task once his tendons have severed apart and his muscles have turned pulpy with decay. But perhaps you will not fail—"

I wanted to kill him.

My fists were knotted at my sides, and I yearned to spring across his desk and clamp my hands over his throat, to eradicate him from existence; to consign him forthwith to whatever afterlife served the dregs of mankind. But I could not. Hideous as it was, I had a duty to Sam Cooper. In that, Mallory was right. If I could pluck the secret process from the runic inscriptions, perhaps Sam could be saved. Saved? A strange word. My mind reeled with the concept, the sheer horror. Perhaps my body swayed. Mallory was regarding me strangely. Then I saw he was not looking at me, but rather beyond me, at the door. I turned quickly, fearing God knows what, in terror of what loomed upon the threshold.

But it was Arabella.

She stood pale, trembling.

"I'm sorry you overheard," Mallory chided. "You don't understand—"

"You would have done that to me?" she asked.

"My dear—"

"You'd have made me—like Sam?"

Mallory stood up, shaking his head.

"No, no. Not like Sam. Like yourself, forever. I will give you immortality, Arabella. And you, Ashley. We will live forever, we will never die. Can't you see? We will be immortal! We will watch the Earth itself grow old, we will venture to the stars."

Arabella shook her head. Her lips moved soundlessly. She trembled and rushed from the room.

Mallory sighed and turned to me.

"Why will they not understand, Ashley?" he said.

He sounded pitiful, tired, confused.

"I'd better get to work," I stated.

He nodded. I no longer felt hatred. Whatever emotions actuated my sensibilities were too primitive to be expressed. I went back to the workroom, and when I passed the barred door I did not glance at it.

9

They meant nothing, those strange symbols, which could have bearing on Sam Cooper. One by one, as the meanings became clear, it was evident they were magical incantations and mystical formulas, nothing more; means by which gods could be placated or cajoled, perhaps, but no method by which to confound those emissaries of corruption which feasted upon Sam's flesh. A great jumble of discarded and crumbled paper accumulated on desk and floor as I moved rapidly from symbol to symbol, not attempting to make proper translations now but merely abstracting the essence invoked by the sigil.

At length, tired and discouraged and striving mightily not to confront the ultimate implications of failure, I pushed back my chair. Perhaps it was time to attempt deduction rather than doggedly laboring over the papyrus. But I didn't know where to start. I am no chemist, no doctor, no—a grim thought—mortician. If the process were not spelled out in the runic writings, there was no help I could offer. Well, there was one thing, that was all. I could give Sam peace, as Mallory had destroyed the dead man in Haiti. But I balked at this alternative on two counts: the first was that it would be akin to murder; the second that it might not be possible, for I feared Sam with all the icy chill of horror. Could I persuade Mallory to destroy his living brain? I was doubtful. Was there some intermediate answer? Could he, perhaps, be frozen in a hyper-cold solution, granted some form of cryogenic suspension which would yield us further time? I considered that seriously. But it would mean revealing the truth, which Mallory would not endure, for such would entail legal complications impossible to unravel in the time we had.

I felt absolutely helpless. When I addressed the papyrus once more my eyes were blurred, and I could hardly see the document. It no longer seemed important, merely the superstitious rituals of the dark past, chirographic adumbrations from the Middle Kingdom. Suddenly a chord resounded in my mind and suggested something I should have considered before. During the Middle Kingdom religious freedom had been granted to the masses; the rites of mummification could be claimed by all people, even the peasants, although of course the ruling classes had more elaborate funerals simply because they could afford them. I glanced at the mummy case. I hadn't bothered with the inscriptions carved upon it and thoughtlessly had assumed that Encephalon was a high priest or minor pharaoh. I now perceived that was not necessarily true, although it seemed unimportant; his station in life could not alter the fact—the living fact—within his skull. Or was I overlooking some obvious point? Something dimly realized nagged at me; something to do with all the other mummies I had seen in Egypt, in museums, in the field; some negative fact I should grasp.

I started to fill my pipe.

It came to me then.

The priests, the pharaohs, the nobility contemporary with Encephalon, had not been preserved as he had! They rather had been disemboweled and brained. Why, then, had Encephalon been treated differently? What great man had he been, what hero, what mortal god, to merit an immortality denied even the kings? What magician, sorcerer, necromancer, to be granted more than the pharaohs themselves?

I rose and walked over to the mummy case.

The lid was inscribed with incantations and symbols, but I ignored them and instead examined the side where the lid opened. The coffin had been sealed with an elaborate inscription; broken with the opening, the writing fitted together again with the case closed. I traced the hieroglyphs with my forefinger, then cursed myself for a fool. I had been seeking knowledge hidden in runic designs, while all the time that knowledge was carved here in simplicity. The message had not been hidden or obscured; it could not have been more apparent, there for all to see, intended for all to see. It was not only written in hieratic but in the simpler demotic, reiterated to insure it would not be misunderstood. Nor did I fail to understand it.

I also understood Mallory's terrible mistake.

Arabella was poised on the stairs, one hand clutching the bannister, like a cat that has clawed its way up a tree and is afraid to descend. I paused. She motioned to me silently. The door to Mallory's study was closed. I walked over to the stairs.

"Is it true, those things he said?"

"Yes," I told her.

She bit her lip.

"You can't mean to be a part of this, Thomas."

"No. I had to try—if there was some way. But no."

"Take me away with you."

"Of course."

"Lucian—might not like it."

I shrugged.

"Is he insane, Thomas?"

"I don't know."

"I want to leave now, right now."

"I have to explain something to Mallory first."

"I'm frightened."

"Get your bags packed, if you will."

She gestured, knifing the air. Her possessions were not important.

"All right. Wait in your room. I'll be ready in a few minutes."

"Be careful, Thomas."

"There's nothing to worry about."

"But—Sam—"

"He's safely locked away."

"Just be careful," she admonished.

Mallory started abruptly as I entered. My face felt stiff, I must have looked grim. He studied me for a moment, then blurted, "Well? What is it?" I shook my head. "Have you found anything?"

"Something—"

"Then we must hurry. What is it, the formula, the—"

"Not what you imagined."

"Is something wrong?"

"Something has been wrong for a long time, Mallory. Say, four thousand years. Mallory, there is no secret process for preserving the body. It can be dried, tanned like leather, but not kept as in life."

"But—there must be."

I shook my head.

"There has to be, Ashley. It wouldn't make sense otherwise."

"You'd better come down to the workroom. I've something to show you."

He rose deliberately, hands on the desk, then came around with an agitated stride. We slowly descended to the workroom without speaking. The bar across Sam's door seemed very prominent, as if the new metal gathered whatever light was available in the dark corridor. We entered the workroom. Mallory watched me, his face heavy with worry and doubt. All the assemblage of ikons and statues watched me. It would have been a dramatic situation, but for the overriding horror. Mallory moved toward the desk, but I went on to the mummy case. After a moment he followed me.

"Did it never occur to you that the priests and the pharaohs were not prepared as Encephalon was?" I asked. "They were brained and gutted. Why did you imagine they were denied the immortality granted your lowborn mummy?"

He looked amazed. "Why, I never considered that. It didn't seem— Do you know why?"

"Yes, Mallory. I know why."

He looked back and forth between me and the mummy case.

"Better oblivion than such eternity," I stated.

"What are you saying?"

I touched the broken seal.

"Shall I translate?"

Mallory nodded.

The message was already seared in my consciousness, and I had no need to concentrate, but I stared at the seal to avoid looking at Mallory. I read it:

Know ye then, despoilers of the grave, that herein lies the archfiend Nistarah, abomination to man and god, condemned to the torment of the ages; be bound then by the curse of Set; disturb not his torment but let him dwell within, denied Life and Underworld, so long as men may walk the earth; such were his sins.

"What does it mean?" Mallory asked.

"Mallory, your mummy was a fiend, a criminal of the highest order; God knows what his sins were. His mind was preserved, yes; preserved in the manner of the foulest defilers of the ancient laws. Immortality was no gift, Mallory! It was a punishment!"

Mallory licked his lips. His eyes darted about as if seeking to bury themselves in his skull. "No," he croaked. "That can't be—in Haiti—"

"In Haiti—that should have been the clue. Not seven years, Mallory. Seven weeks, perhaps. Is it a virtue, to serve your master even after death?"

"No, no, it can't be. You must continue to work, Ashley. The answer must be in the papyrus—"

"There is no answer."

He glared at me. He turned sharply and walked over to the desk, then stood looking down at the rolled script for a moment, leaning on his hands. His shoulders rose and fell, he tilted his head. Suddenly, with an explosive gasp of breath, he snatched up the papyrus and tore it apart. I started toward him instinctively, to prevent the destruction of the ancient document. Then I slowed, as if my feet were reluctant before my mind, my body before my instincts. Let him tear the papyrus apart, I thought; better it had never been found; better that ancient Egypt had been covered by the sands forever than that one man should live as Sam Cooper lived.

Mallory had gone berserk.

He hurled a jade ikon against the wall, swept the desk clear of papers, kicked violently at a packing crate, toppling a faience deity. He seized a heavy idol, a bull-headed god, and seemed about to dash it to the floor. Then he halted and sighed, looking at the statue as if it were the Minotaur at the end of his maze of frustration. He seemed calm enough now. I approached.

He peered at me obliquely.

"There's nothing more I can do," I said.

He remained sullenly silent.

"Give me the keys to your car." I tendered this request in a calm voice, reasonable, logical, wanting no difficulties now. There were sufficient difficulties in the burden of my knowledge.

"What? Why?"

"I want to leave, Mallory."

A sly look registered in his eyes.

"Where will you go?"

"I don't know," I said, and meant it. What could one do? Could a dead man be locked up for a crime? Imprisoned to await a trial while his flesh rotted from his bones? What could anyone do? Peal would not believe me. He might check, but then, the truth known, what next? Would the authorities debate the issue while Sam decomposed into stinking corruption? No, that was not the answer. I said, "Sam must be destroyed, Mallory. Surely you can see that? Will you do it?"

"Destroyed? No! He lives."

"Destroy his brain. You must. If you'll do that, Mallory, I'll say nothing. The evil is done, it cannot be rectified by legal vengeance."

"No, no, you fool. Sam must be studied. Perhaps it is true, perhaps there was no method of preservation, but can we not find one? By studying Sam, others—?"

There was no reasoning with him. The dreams of his lifetime had been shattered—the dreams of far more than a lifetime. I knew it was cowardly, but I had only one thought—to get away from that place. I held out my hand.

"The keys."

"You'll go to the police?"

"Give me the keys, damn you."

"Ashley—no, not with my work undone."

"Your work? Better had it never begun."

I stepped closer, prepared to take the keys by force if necessary, not fearing Mallory physically. He turned pale. He reached into his pocket and brought out the keycase; handed it to me. I started to speak, to say something, perhaps to express regret.

Then Mallory struck me.

He spun sideways, and I saw the blur of the bull-headed idol as it came around. I threw up my forearm, too late, and felt an explosion inside my head. Suddenly I was sitting on the floor, a trickle of blood at my temple. The car keys were on the stones beside me. I blinked and shook my head. Mallory stood back, frightened, peering down the angle of his face. As I started to rise he wheeled and ran. I reached for the keys, not thinking clearly. Let Mallory go, I wanted nothing from him. I heard his footfalls in the corridor. They stopped abruptly, and, in the sudden silence, the truth shrieked within me.

I lurched to my feet and took one staggering step.

"Mallory! No! For God's sake, no!" I screamed.

My cry echoed in the corridor.

Through the echo, I heard the bar clang back from Sam's door—

I was staggering—perhaps from the blow on my head, perhaps from my horror—as I moved toward the door. I still held the car keys, a symbol of salvation clutched before me like a crucifix against a vampire. I knew only one slight hope. Sam could not act quickly, his responses were delayed—if I could get past his cell before his living brain sent impulses to his body—if I could get to the car—

I stumbled into the corridor. Mallory stood there, holding Sam's door back with one hand and, with the other, pointing toward the workroom where I stood. As I stepped into the corridor, he glared at me, his face contorted with malevolence and evil. He shouted some wordless command, the veins in his neck standing out starkly. I had to force my second step, my body cringed from the corridor.

Then it was too late.

Sam lumbered out.

He walked stiffly, bent at the waist, hands hanging limply at his thighs; he came directly out and then turned unerringly toward me. Mallory hovered behind him, still voicing those wordless commands. I took a step backward, Sam lurched on, moving more surely with every step. His hands were huge, heavy, the fingers starting to distort into hooks, while his eyes began to assume a bestial ferocity. His footfalls were rhythmic on the floor.

I retreated back into the workroom, too terrified even to close the door. His bulk blocked the entrance, passed through. I backed against the mummy case and crouched there, my heart volcanic. Sam seemed to have lost sight of me for a moment. He stood inside the door, craning his huge head from side to side, seeking me with his yellow eyes. His stench flowed out before him, and I saw the dripping blotches grained into his face. I looked at Mallory, pleading with my eyes, prepared to beg on my knees, to make any promise, if he would call back this horror. But there was no reprieve in his face. He glowered with triumph, pointing me out. Sam's head swiveled, following Mallory's thrusting forefinger, then stopped, dead eyes fixed upon me. They were the eyes of smoldering sulphur. His mouth opened and he roared, but no sound emerged; without breath, he roared silently. Instead of sound came a terrible emanation of odor, the stench of his rotting guts. He shuffled forward, hands extending, grasping—

I hurled the mummy case between us.

The heavy coffin struck Sam in the chest and plunged down, smashing upright against the floor. The lid burst open and Encephalon flew out like a broken doll, directly into Sam's hands. Sam turned his eyes down. The blackened mummy twisted and flopped in his grasp. Mallory was shouting. Sam seemed confused. Slowly, remorselessly, he tore one shriveled arm from its ancient socket. He shook the dismembered mummy by the throat. I tried to slip by him while he was thus occupied, but he suddenly threw the mummy aside in rage and lunged for me again, intercepting my flight. He was closing in. I quivered against the wall, all strength gone, my muscles turned to fluids. As he reached for my throat, his mouth instinctively dropped open.

A cry tore through the room.

Sam could make no sound.

It was Arabella, screaming at the door.

She shocked me from the stupor of fear.

"Run," I cried. "Arabella, run!"

But she stood there. She cried out again. Suddenly I realized it was not a scream of terror, that she was voicing words, a plea, a command.

And Sam had halted.

With his putrescent fingers inches from my throat, he stopped. His massive body quivered, his eyes glazed, the blemished skin of his brow drew up in deep creases. "Sam!" she cried. "Sam, no! Sam!" Ponderously, he turned toward her. His shoulder brushed against me. "Leave him alone, Sam!" she shouted. Mallory too was shouting. He glared with hatred at Arabella. Sam trembled. I saw his monstrous face in profile; saw—most terrible of all—human indecision writhing on the countenance of a corpse.

Mallory gasped with comprehension. He had not believed Sam capable of emotion, or decision. Snarling, he rushed at Arabella. She flinched away as he seized her. He slammed her back against the wall and his long fingers reached to her throat, to stifle her cries, to eradicate the indecision tormenting his hideous creation.

But Mallory had moved too late.

As his hands clutched Arabella's throat, Sam reared and lurched forward. Mallory heard him coming. He looked back over his shoulder and his mouth dropped open. Terror transfused his face. The door was there beside him, but he was frozen in place, watching that which he had created advance upon him. He released Arabella and held both hands before him, palms open. Sam took him in his arms. Slowly, almost tenderly, he turned Mallory from the wall, bending him back, bending over him. They sank to the floor together, coupled in embrace. Mallory uttered no sound as Sam's savage face lowered to him.

I waited to see no more.

I don't remember our flight from that room, from the house. It was a frenzied retreat through a void. Awareness did not return until we stood outside, beside the car. Arabella was sobbing against my chest. I had one arm around her shoulders, the other on the door handle. The moon had risen, and the world transformed into a palely translucent chiaroscuro. I had become very cold, very composed now. There is a limit to the emotions the human mind can endure. Arabella was releasing hers in tears; I had frozen mine in ice. I took my hand from the door and held her in both arms. She felt very fragile. I was looking beyond her, at the woodpile. In the moonlight, the woodpile too was cold. It seemed carved from a block of ice. The axe stood upright and cast a long shadow. The shadow pointed at me.

Presently, Arabella drew back and gazed at me, trembling, questioning.

"I have to go back," I said.

"Yes, I know."

"I can't just leave him like that."

"I know, Thomas."

"Lock yourself in the car."

"I'll come with you."

I shook my head.

"But, Thomas—I have to." She was wide-eyed, logical. "You can see that. I can control him. He'd kill you alone. But he—you saw—he obeyed me. He helped me." She trembled violently with those words. But it was true. It was the most terrible part of all, but true. Arabella was right. Sam might be uncontrollable now, he might kill both of us, but there are things worse than death. I nodded. She tried to smile. I grasped the axe.

Sam was still crouched over Mallory's body.

We saw him from the door. It was not an occasion for the traditions of bravery, and I let Arabella step first into the room. She stood just inside the door and spoke his name, softly. After what seemed a long time, Sam gaped upward, crooking his head sideways.

The fury was gone from his eyes now, his jaw dripped strands of gore. Arabella's shoulders quivered as she saw his face, but she didn't look away. And slow, very slowly, Sam's expression changed. His face drew upward at the mouth.

Arabella gasped.

Dutiful, faithful, pleased to have served her, Sam Cooper was smiling.

Impaled upon that smile, Arabella swayed.

Sam lowered his face once more to Mallory.

Arabella closed her eyes. Sam did not appear to notice me as I moved past Arabella and into the room, holding the axe across my chest. I took my stance behind him, my feet spread wide. I couldn't see his face from there, and I didn't wish to. That terrible smile had been incised into my soul. But I could see the arched back of his neck. I shifted my weight and lifted the axe at the angle. Sam's head moved from side to side on Mallory's body. I hesitated, but only for a moment; only to gauge the distance. There was no moral problem here to be judged.

This was no murder.

The murder already had been committed.

This was simply the final rites.

There was little blood.

Blood does not rush forth when no heart beats. My blow was true, and Sam's head fell to the side, rebounding twice and turning over. His body, as if long awaiting this moment, collapsed instantly and seemed to deflate and flatten, boneless and liquescent. I had to take two steps, slow and steady, before I stood over the severed head. It rested face upward on the stones. The eyes were open, Sam stared up at me, for a moment our gaze locked. Perhaps he understood, then. Freed of his body, he may have known. I like to tell myself that he did, that the look he raised to me from his disembodied head was one of gratitude. I finished the task deliberately, not stopping until the axe blade was ringing on the stones and nothing remained there without purpose to a corpse.

The task finished, I began to tremble.

My bones rattled.

I had barely enough strength left for Encephalon, but he was old, old, and the effort was small. Done, I hurled the axe aside and leaned against the operating table, my head lowered, twitching spasmodically. Arabella came to stand behind me and touched my shoulder. I raised my face. The ikons and idols leered at me from the shelves, preserving their timeless vigil. Each and every one out of Egypt, they all represented immortality. I cursed them blasphemously, savagely. Arabella, startled, stepped back. But the ikons and idols did not move at all. Manifestations of immortality, they were motionless forever.

It was Arabella who suggested I wipe my fingerprints from the axe. At first I couldn't apprehend her meaning. I had no sense of having committed a crime. But slowly the facts came clear. The truth was impossible; it would never be believed. To admit to what I had done, I could only plead self-defense, but with the absolute destruction I had authored, it would be a feeble defense indeed. My mind began to function again. As I considered obliterating my fingerprints, it came to me that far more than the marks of my hands should be removed from this room; rather removed from the memory of mankind. I began shoving and hauling the packing crates and tables into the center of the room. Arabella understood my purpose immediately. She assisted me, keeping her eyes averted from the bodies. I added the mummy case to the burgeoning pile with reluctance, but determination. Mallory's relics were ancient and dry, they would burn well. Many of the chemicals were combustible, and I poured them over the wood. I placed the papyrus last atop the pile. It was the sum of Mallory's knowledge, offered up beside his corpse. Mallory's knowledge, too, was ancient. It was as old and as dry as his relics. It would also burn well.

We left the house together, hand in hand. Already we could hear the flames crackling from within. It was better that Mallory's car remained, and we walked down the drive toward the road. Halfway there, my emotions overwhelmed me and I had to pause, leaning against the stone fence. Arabella still held my hand. She was watching me, tight-lipped, wide-eyed. I told her I'd be all right in a moment and pressed her hand. She returned the gesture. We were coupled by more than a handclasp, locked together by the knowledge we shared. Perhaps we were joined for a lifetime. I looked at her. I was older than she, but having stared into the jaws of eternity, I realized that the fleeting years seemed insignificant. One lives a span, one grows old, one dies. That is as it should be. Exactly as it should be. I smiled, and Arabella smiled back. Perhaps she was sharing my thoughts. At that moment the first flames blazed into the night.

We both turned back.

The fire had burst from the narrow window of the workroom, raging up the wall in a fiery conflagration. Black smoke was roiling from the other side of the house, and in a moment the fire roared there too. The seething smoke was shot through with fierce red flames. For a few minutes this furious tableau was maintained: one hook on either side of the house, like a burning hand holding the structure upright in its palm. The smoke plumed and billowed upward, obscuring the angles of the house but leaving the peaked roof starkly resplendent in the cold moonlight. It made the building seem angular, wedge-shaped. I felt that I had experienced the impression before, but only afterward did its significance become apparent to me. The blazing structure eerily resembled a pyramid thrusting up from the desert, built to last forever, a monumental mockery of mortal dreams.